"You look surprised to see *me*, Quinn."

Tilting her head, Daeva looked him up and down. "Oh, that's right. You never did get to see me in my true form. You were so quick to get rid of me. Never gave me a chance to introduce myself properly."

It had been three years since Daeva had seen Quinn Strom. And she had to admit that he looked just as dark and dangerous and delicious. His inner darkness called to her like a moth to a flame. But she couldn't let him see that. She couldn't let him have the upper hand here. She'd never give it to him again.

SEDUCING THE HUNTER

VIVI ANNA

MILLS & BOON

Published in Great Britain 2014
by Mills & Boon, an imprint of Harlequin (UK) Limited,
Eton House, 18-24 Paradise Road, Richmond, Surrey, TW9 1SR

© 2014 Vivi Anna

ISBN: 978-0-263-91414-6

89-1214

Harlequin (UK) Limited's policy is to use papers that are natural, renewable and recyclable products and made from wood grown in sustainable forests. The logging and manufacturing processes conform to the legal environmental regulations of the country of origin.

Printed and bound in Spain
by CPI, Barcelona

A vixen at heart, **Vivi Anna** likes to burn up the pages with her original, unique brand of fantasy fiction. Whether it's in the Amazon jungle, an apocalyptic future or the otherworld city of Necropolis, Vivi always writes fast-paced action-adventure with strong, independent women who can kick some butt and dark, delicious heroes to kill for.

Once shot at while repossessing a car, Vivi decided that maybe her life needed a change. The first time she picked up a pen and put words to paper, she knew she had found her heart's desire. Within two paragraphs, she realized she could write about getting into all sorts of trouble without having to suffer any of the consequences.

When Vivi isn't writing, you can find her causing a ruckus at downtown bistros, flea markets or in her own backyard.

For Crowley,
the cheekiest demon of them all…

Chapter 1

The candlelight illuminating the small chamber flickered when the heavy wooden door opened. Daeva looked up from the backgammon board to see who had entered her private room. She smiled as the little green creature, carrying a bronze tea tray, hobbled in on his spindly and knobby legs.

He set the tray on the small round table next to her, then slid onto the velvet-covered chair on the opposite side of the backgammon board.

She reached over and poured tea into two

porcelain cups then handed one to him. "Prompt as usual, Klix."

The creature accepted the offered cup and took a sip, his beady black eyes staring at her over the rim. "I wouldn't miss our daily game, Mistress."

She drank the hot, spiced tea and watched the goblin set up the game. It was her one small pleasure in the day, to play the ordinary game with him in her private chamber away from the others. Away from the reality of her situation.

Here she couldn't smell the rancid odor of brimstone and sulfur or the stench of burning flesh. Here she could block out the woeful screams and pitiful mewls of those being tortured in the fire pits below. She didn't have to make polite conversation with the other demons she wholly despised. As long as she had to stay in hell, she could at least pretend she was elsewhere when she was here in her room playing her games with her friend Klix.

Hell was the place of Daeva's birth, but she'd done everything possible for thousands of years to get out and stay out. And she'd done pretty well. Staying topside most of her life, possessing bodies, living their lives, until some clever exorcist or demon hunter would exorcise her back to hell. Then the process would start all over again. It wasn't perfect but she'd accepted the fact that she'd never be able to walk the mortal realm in her true form, so she'd stolen identities and pretended to be those people. It wasn't quite like being a real mortal. But it was the best she could do in her circumstances.

At least when she took over a body, she kept her host in a dream state. They didn't know they were being possessed. They just thought they were having one heck of an amazing dream. Daeva always gave them good, happy dreams.

Despite what a lot of lore said, not all demons were wicked. In fact, most lived, just as other beings did, somewhere between good and evil. Here, in hell, demons were split into seven types. Daeva was of the second, which consisted of lust demons. She wasn't a full-blooded lust demon though; there had been some mixing of types over millennia, but she had one in the family tree somewhere. She didn't possess people to just suck the sexual energy from them or those that they seduced. She wasn't what some people would call a succubus.

But she did derive some energy from sex.

Which was one of the reasons she preferred to possess the bodies of women. She liked sex with men. She supposed her affinity to them was one of her weaknesses. She'd been told as much by every other demon in her family tree. Which was one of the many reasons she hated it so much in hell.

She'd been doing okay as a mortal for years, surviving, forging a pretty good new life with a job, a home, friends, family and a man she loved. The woman whom she'd possessed had been near death in a coma when Daeva had come along. Her brain had little function so it would've been like being in a dream for her when Daeva had taken over. The girl was mercifully unaware of Daeva's presence. But that all had come to a halt about three years ago when she'd been exorcised out of her most favorite body, her most favorite life, and sent back to this…hell. She'd been looking for a way back ever since.

She'd been looking for payback on the man who'd sent her back, who just happened to be the same man she'd loved.

Klix had the game set up—he always played the black—then picked up the dice and rolled.

She watched him move the pieces with his crooked fingers and smiled. He was her only comfort in a place that offered nothing but misery and suffering.

"So, my friend, what is the word out in the world?" she asked as she took her turn.

"Loir is going topside," he said as he rolled again.

"Really?" This surprised Daeva. Loir was Klix's twin sister. Goblins usually didn't go to the mortal realm. They weren't very good at assimilating into the human world. Seeing a four-foot, bald, green-skinned creature with bulbous eyes, razor-sharp talons and four sets of teeth would send anyone into a panic or an asylum. "What is her purpose?"

Klix shrugged. "I am not sure. She would not tell me much."

"She must be accompanying someone on a task."

He nodded. "Yes, that would be logical." He moved some of his black pieces into the winning box. "She did say something about a key."

This perked Daeva up. There were only a few important keys up there in the world. "What kind of key, do you know?"

"Not sure. But I did hear it is supposed to open something of great value to demons. Something powerful. Something ancient."

Daeva nearly dropped her teacup. She set it on the table, her hand shaking.

"Are you ill, Mistress?"

She swallowed, then gave him a small smile. "I must be a bit under the weather, Klix. Could we finish our game later? I believe I need to rest a bit."

"Yes, of course." He rose from his seat. "Shall I take the tea tray?"

"No, that's fine."

He bowed his bald head to her. "I will be back later to check on you, Mistress."

"Oh, Klix, could you deliver a message to your sister for me?" Daeva reached for parchment and a quill. She scrawled three words on it, and folded the paper. She handed it to the goblin.

"I will do this right away."

"Thank you, Klix. Please tell her to burn it after she reads it."

The little goblin left her chamber, shutting the door firmly behind him.

Once he was gone, Daeva rose from her chair

and went to the floor-to-ceiling bookcase along one wall. She ran her finger along the book titles until she found the one she needed. She slid it off the shelf and went to sit on the sofa.

She opened the thick tome on her lap and flipped through the pages. She stopped at a picture of a large wooden box with an elaborate lock on it. She read the text that went with it, then her finger circled another picture, that of a key. A skeleton key. The key that fit the lock. The key that opened a box that had been buried.

A plain wooden box she had buried herself, over a hundred years ago.

She sighed and leaned back against the sofa cushions. She prayed that this wasn't the key Loir had gone topside to look for. As far as she knew, she was one of only a few people who knew who had the key. If someone was looking for it, then they were looking for the box.

The box had been entrusted to her more than a century ago by an elderly human scholar. He'd been an intelligent, well-read man who knew about the curse on the box. He knew exactly what had been sealed inside. And he had pleaded with her to bury it where no one, no human, no demon, would be able to find it again. He had been her friend, one of the few she had as a demon, so she did as he asked. With the help of a local man, she'd buried it deep in the earth in northern Canada.

They couldn't allow what lay inside the box to be used again. Daeva feared what would happen if it fell into demon hands. It had been used against demonkind two millennia ago, used to enslave them and do one insane man's bidding. But if it fell into demon hands, it could be used to subjugate the entire human population. It would overthrow humanity.

Recently, she had heard rumors and whispers about who possessed the key. And the last confirmed report had chilled her blood. If only she was still topside, she could've protected him, the key keeper, and he would never have even known.

Because she'd spent years right under his nose, hiding in plain sight. Hiding inside the woman he'd fallen in love with. The woman she'd been possessing for years, before she even met him. So, in Daeva's mind, he had fallen in love with her.

And she had loved him. Damn him for it.

She pushed the book to the side and stood.

Pacing the room she flicked her hand and all the candles in her chamber lit. She tried to warm her body with their flames. It would surprise everyone to know that even in hell she could be cold. She worried about what was to come, fretted about the future.

Daeva knew she would be called upon. There was only one being still alive who knew she'd hidden the box. The man she'd loved, the man who had sent her back to hell.

Soon, Quinn Strom, exorcist extraordinaire, would come a-knocking at her hellish "door."

A knock startled her. It couldn't be Klix; she had told him to come back later. Her heart thudding in her chest, she opened the door.

Two soldiers with swords at their sides stood waiting for her. "Daeva, you must come with us."

"What is this about?" Although, deep down in her churning gut, she knew.

"Please comply, or we will be forced to be unpleasant."

Swallowing the fear that was quickly rising, she nodded and stepped out between them, firmly shutting her door behind her.

Chapter 2

The sound was faint, maybe only a creak of the house, but Quinn Strom heard it. He sat upright in his bed, peering into the darkness of his bedroom and straining to listen.

Trained to sleep lightly, he was always alert at any out-of-place sound. He'd lived in his modest house long enough to have memorized every normal creak, squeak and groan of the place. And the creak he'd heard was from the stairs just outside his room; the fourth step from the top had a soft spot that only a certain amount of weight triggered.

The creak came again, prompting Quinn to bolt off the bed and reach under his bed for the arsenal that he'd stashed there when he first moved in. Fortunately he always slept in sweat-pants, so in emergencies like these he didn't have to bother dressing. He grabbed the shot-gun, loaded with silver and rock salt, and the beat-up old satchel that contained ampoules of holy water and his blessed silver crucifix.

Quinn had been a demon hunter and exorcist for most of his life, so he was always prepared for any threat, be it human or other. His father had trained him since he was ten to be vigi-lant, to be wary of the things that went bump in the night.

All the doors and windows had been warded against demon attacks, so the intruder had to be human. But just because they were human didn't make them any less of a threat. He knew that firsthand. He'd had his fair share of run-ins with sorcerers, especially those from the Crim-son Hall Cabal, a powerful organization of one hundred members who were always searching for more power.

Quinn took position at the side of his door, his gun raised, the satchel hung over his shoul-

der. He couldn't cock the gun now because of
the sound it would make, but the moment the
door opened, he would pump it and point it in
a nanosecond. In his other hand he had a glass
ampoule of holy water ready to be released, just
in case his wards had failed. One splash of the
water on unholy skin would incapacitate any
demon for a few minutes. Enough time for him
to shoot silver into a demon body and kill it.

Breathing deep and even, he counted down
the seconds in his head. The attack would come
any moment now. He could sense movement on
the other side of the door, hear the swish of fabric moving. What the hell were they waiting for?

Could this be a regular, run-of-the-mill home
burglar? Looking for expensive things to steal
and hock? Quinn didn't live in an affluent
neighborhood. There was no indication in either his house decor or the vehicle he drove that
he was anything but a blue-collar working man
with nothing of worth to take except maybe a
plasma TV and a game console. But nothing
worth searching the rest of the house for.

No, Quinn didn't harbor any delusions that
the intruders were after his valuables. At least,
not the type that a person could buy in a de-

partment store. He did possess some things of worth. Things that only certain types of humans and demons would know about.

Were they after the key? God, he hoped not. That thing had been nothing but trouble from the second his father had bequeathed it to him. He'd tried to hide it in plain sight by giving it to his sister disguised as a pendant, but it had ended up back in his hands anyway. Back to being his responsibility.

Before he could consider that further, the door burst open. And not in one push. It splintered into a hundred pieces, as if C-4 had been placed on it and lit by a fuse. But he didn't hear an explosion. Something else of great power had rendered his door into kindling.

He cocked the shotgun and, stepping over the wood pieces scattered on his floor, he took a stance in the doorway, pointing his weapon. But he couldn't get a shot off before he was catapulted backward by a ball of green light that hit him full force in the gut. All the air was knocked out of him when he hit the wall.

He slumped to the floor just as a man with long dark hair and glowing green hands stepped into his bedroom. He smiled down at Quinn.

"Quinn Strom, I presume. Where is the key?"

All of Quinn's muscles quivered. It was as if a thousand volts of electricity surged through his body. He could barely blink.

The man stood over him, threatening green sparks dripping like melted metal from his long fingers. "I don't want to kill you. But I will to get what I want."

Quinn licked his lips, trying to get his mouth to work. "I don't know what you're talking about."

"Don't play with me, Strom. I know you have it. Your lovely sister, Ivy, had it and then she gave it to you."

Quinn tried to sit up at the mention of Ivy's name. "If you touched her, I'll kill you."

The man chuckled. "Don't worry, she is quite safe. The cambion of hers is quite formidable. I should know, he killed Reginald, the man I succeeded as leader of the Cabal." He turned his glowing hands this way and that, looking at them affectionately. "Although I probably should thank him for that…"

Quinn now knew who had broken into his house. The Crimson Hall Cabal. They were a ruthless group of powerful sorcerers who ran their organization pretty much like the mob and a gentlemen's club combined. Not long ago, his sister, Ivy, and her lover, Ronan, a cambion, otherwise known as a half demon, had had a run-in with Reginald Watson. He'd initially hired Ronan to find Quinn and steal the key. But Ronan had had a change of heart—everything to do with the fact that he'd fallen in love with Ivy—and had given the key back. Then he ended up killing Reginald to keep Ivy and the key safe.

Obviously, the legend of the key had been passed on to the next in line for the cabal throne. The legend and the desire to possess it.

"You've wasted a trip. I don't have the key," Quinn croaked, his throat dry from the pain that still zipped through his body.

There was movement behind the sorcerer in the doorway. He turned as a small squat creature hobbled into the room.

"I could not find it, Master."

It was a goblin, a female one by the way it was shaped. It regarded Quinn with its big, opaque eyes, and Quinn thought maybe he saw a quick flash of remorse in its wide-eyed stare. He couldn't be sure. He'd only ever seen a goblin once before. It was rare to see one topside. They usually resided in hell, acting as servants to the demons that inhabited the pits.

"Yes, well, I did not suspect that the great Quinn Strom would have it lying around." The sorcerer looked back to him. "You're much too much like your father. Paranoid to a fault. Too bad that didn't help him before he died."

"I'd leave my dad out of this."

"Or what?" the sorcerer sneered. "You're going to kill me?"

Quinn nodded. "Something like that." He pulled his hand out of his satchel and a dagger glinted in the light cast by the sorcerer's hands. The sorcerer saw the knife too late.

He lifted his hands, just as Quinn sank the lethal blade into the sorcerer's leg, and dodged his magic green rays. The green light slammed into the wall behind him, just missing his head, and burned a hole through the wood and concrete.

Dragging the shotgun with him, Quinn gained his feet, but the sorcerer was already turning toward him, the knife still sticking out of his thigh. Quinn dashed past the little goblin and out of the room. A blast of green fire hit him in the shoulder as he rounded the doorway.

It sent him to the ground, and he rolled dangerously close to the first step on the staircase. Pain shot through him like acid, but he managed to pull himself up using the railing and started down the stairs. Another bolt of green hit the wall next to him, causing him to stumble. Sparks sizzled on his cheek.

He reached the bottom step just as the sorcerer started down. Quinn risked a glance at him. The sorcerer had pulled the knife from his leg and dark droplets splattered the rug with each step he took. It wouldn't be long before the blood loss affected the sorcerer's vision. He'd be seeing black spots soon. Or least, Quinn hoped he would.

Quinn ran into the living room. He had to get to his bookcase. There was one book he needed before he could get out of the house. The room had been trashed by the little goblin. Sofa cushions had been sliced open and spilled out on the floor. All his shelves were tossed. The bookcase was broken apart on the rug, the books scattered everywhere.

He surveyed the damage, desperately seeking a thick black tome. He spied it in the corner, off by itself. As if waiting for him.

He dashed for it even as the sorcerer came around the corner, his hands glowing brighter. Quinn had a feeling that if he was hit by another wave of magic he wasn't going to be getting up so easily. He'd crossed paths with the sorcerers before, but this one's magic seemed much more powerful.

Ducking to grab the book, he barely missed being hit by a large orb of green. It crashed into the wall just above him. Liquid green sparks rained down on him, burning holes in his skin. He sucked in a breath to deal with the pain and shoved the book into his satchel.

If he could just make it to the kitchen, he could escape out the back. He had an escape route planned in advance. One he'd practiced repeatedly. He'd dash across the yard, out the back gate, down the alley and over the fence of his neighbors who had two dogs he'd already made friends with. After going through their yard, out the front and down another block, he'd get to the old junker he had sitting there. The keys were sitting on the right front wheel, under the fender.

But the thoughts were moot. Just as he

reached the archway to the kitchen, he felt the impact on his back.

Quinn catapulted forward. Luckily he had the presence of mind to put his hands out, so he didn't land on his face. But he did manage to smash his knee against the kitchen island as he fell. Dark, searing pain surged over his back, up his neck and over his skull. His vision wavered.

He tried to gain his feet, but dizziness seized him and he collapsed to his knees, agony bursting through the one he'd just battered. "Damn it!" he yelled.

He half crawled, half pulled himself on his stomach, toward the back door. But it was pointless. He was down.

"Admirable, Strom. But face it, I have more power than you do."

Quinn rolled onto his back to see the sorcerer limp into the kitchen, the little goblin trailing behind him.

"Loir, grab the bag."

The little green creature shuffled past the sorcerer to where Quinn was sprawled out on the kitchen floor. He clutched the satchel to his chest. "Touch it, goblin, and I'll bite your hand off."

The goblin grinned at him, showing off four rows of pointed, razor-sharp teeth. "Not before I bite yours off, first."

The sorcerer laughed.

The goblin reached for the bag, but Quinn wouldn't relinquish his hold on it. The creature dragged one sharp talon across the back of Quinn's hand. His skin split open, bubbling with infection.

"Jesus!" he dropped the bag and cradled his injured hand. The pain was intense. It made his head swim. Nausea filled his mouth.

The creature took the bag and handed it to the sorcerer, then shuffled in beside its master.

The sorcerer pulled open the leather bag, and withdrew a Holy Bible. He smiled when he saw it. "Cute."

The sorcerer opened it and flipped through the pages until, Quinn imagined, he came across Quinn's hiding spot. He'd hollowed out pages of the book and set the key inside.

The sorcerer tossed the Bible aside, and held up what he'd found between the pages. It was the key. The key that had been entrusted to Quinn to keep hidden. The key that unlocked the Chest of Sorrows, which contained a book that could end the world.

The sorcerer closed his hand around it. "Thank you, Quinn. Give my best to the demon horde when you get to hell." He turned on his boot heel and glanced down at the goblin. "Make it quick. We have places to be."

"Next time we meet, sorcerer, I'm going to bury that blade in your neck and watch you bleed out," Quinn said.

The sorcerer shook his head with a little smile at his lips. "So much drama, exorcist."

He hobbled out of the kitchen and Quinn could hear his steps through the living room and out the front door, leaving Quinn alone with the little assassin.

The goblin tilted its head and looked at Quinn. "I have longed to meet you, Quinn Strom."

"Is that right?" Quinn cradled his hand to his chest. The infectious bubbling hadn't stopped. The wound had widened and blood joined the phlegmy green liquid oozing out of his hand.

"You are most famous in hell."

Quinn imagined he was. He'd exorcised hundreds of demons back to the fiery pits. He imagined he was hell's Most Wanted. He wondered if there were posters of him nailed to the walls. He hoped they got his good side.

The goblin neared him, regarding him curiously. "Are you afraid to die?"

Quinn boldly met its gaze. "No. Are you?"

"Is there anything you want to say before it happens?"

He nodded. "Yeah, who was that sorcerer bastard?"

"His name is Richter Collins." It smiled, then reached for him.

The goblin squeezed Quinn's head between its mottled green hands. Quinn could feel the scaly skin on his cheeks. It leaned down and looked him straight in the eyes.

"I will not kill you. She would hate it and I will not do that to her, although you have done worse to her, I think."

"Who are you talking about?"

"You know who. The one you wronged. The one you loved, once upon a time. I am one of her loyal servants."

"And she sent you to get her revenge?" he spat.

The goblin shook her head. "No, to save you, stupid man."

Before Quinn could respond, everything went dark.

Chapter 3

"Who has the key?"

"I'm sure I don't know what you are talking about." Daeva pulled at the brown leather straps binding her to the iron chair. They were secure and she didn't think any amount of wriggling was going to get her out of them. The torture room—there really wasn't any reason not to call it that—was small and stifling, with no color anywhere except the dark brown stains on the stone that could be nothing but old blood.

Her torturer loomed over her, a maniacal

gleam in his inky black eyes. "Don't bother. You can't escape. Where would you go? Topside?"

"Well, you can't blame a girl for trying, now, can you?"

He circled the chair that was bolted to the stone floor, leering at her, cleaning under his talons with the tip of the silver blade clasped in his hand. She wondered when he was going to use it on her. Likely after the theatrics. Lord Klaven did enjoy his drama.

"You'd like to go back topside, wouldn't you, Daeva?" he sneered. "To live like a human."

"Better than living like an animal like you, Klaven."

He chuckled, and it chilled her to the bone. "But you are like me, Daeva. I remember the fun we used to have together."

"That was millennia ago."

"True." He leaned into her face, and she could smell the rotten meat on his breath. "But they were so deliciously twisted that I remember them like it was yesterday." He licked his lips. "You were one depraved woman."

"Were is the operative word here. I'm not that person anymore."

"True." He straightened and regarded her

with contempt. "Now you are weak and human tainted." He sniffed the air. "You still smell like the exorcist, even after all this time. Did you steal some of his clothing when he sent you back?"

She winced inside at the mention of Quinn. It still hurt to think of him.

"Although he didn't want you, now, did he?"

She glared at him. "Come closer and say that."

He laughed again, then twirled the blade between his fingers. "Oh, poor Daeva. Exorcised by the man you loved. At least, that's what I heard. Is it true?" He leaned down into her face.

She turned away. She didn't want to look into his vacant eyes, didn't want to see the total lack of empathy or emotion there.

"Oh, you're not going to cry are you?" He drew the blade tip across her lips. "I do so hate to see a lady shed tears. Especially over a man who tossed her away like the heathen she is."

Klaven took a step back, and the air shimmered around him until it was Quinn standing in front of her and not the demon lord. The fake Quinn image smiled.

"It must've hurt when he banished you." He took a step toward her.

She didn't look at him, she stared at the stained floor. She couldn't see Quinn looking at her like that, not again. As if she was an animal. As if she wasn't a woman but pure filth.

"Did he torture you first? Did he sprinkle holy water on you? Burning your flesh, burning your soul."

She didn't rise to the bait, although she remembered that night three years ago when Quinn exorcised her as though it had just happened. It was still fresh and raw in her mind. And being reminded of it by the horrid Lord Klaven didn't help matters. Her stomach churned at the memory.

He moved closer to her again, gripping her chin with his long, bony fingers. He lifted her head up, forcing her to look upon him. She wanted to scream at seeing Quinn's face with black eyes and fangs poking out between his full lips. Lips she used to kiss for hours on end.

"Does the exorcist have the key?"

She spat at him.

Klaven wiped the spittle from his cheek, then grinned down at her. "Does he have the chest?"

"You're wasting your time, Klaven. I won't tell you anything. You can't kill me, so you might as well let me go."

He wrapped a hand in her hair and pulled her head back, exposing her neck. Leaning down, he slammed his mouth on hers, kissing her fiercely. She bit his tongue when it invaded her mouth. His sulfur-tainted blood filled her mouth.

He jerked away, his crimson-stained lips pulling back into an evil sneer. "I might not be allowed to kill you, Daeva. But I certainly can have my fun."

He drew his knife down her arm, slicing open her skin. She bit down on her lip to stop from crying out at the pain. She looked down at her damaged flesh, knowing his demon-cursed blade would leave a scar and that she would use that as a reminder of this day. Of Klaven's betrayal—and that of all of the demon horde.

"Do your worst. I do not fear you or anything that you can do to me."

Klaven, still looking like Quinn, clapped his hands, and the heavy metal door opened. The two guards that had brought her here marched in.

"Grab her and tie her to the rack."

When they came to unbind her, she kicked and struggled and lashed out at them, but they were twice her strength. There was nothing she could do when they dragged her across the room to the ancient wooden rack that was once owned by the Marquis de Sade, a close personal friend of Klaven's.

Her torture was going to be savage. She'd seen Klaven's artwork before. But she swore to herself she would hold out as long as she could. No matter what Quinn had done to her all those years ago, she still didn't want to see him harmed. And if the demons knew he possessed the key, he would not be safe. His death would be her fault.

Chapter 4

When Quinn finally woke, the sun was streaming in through the big kitchen and his head was pounding something fierce.

He made his way to his knees, then up to his feet, using the kitchen counter to brace himself against. His hand still throbbed where the goblin had wounded him, but it was no longer oozing with infectious goo or blood. It still needed tending to, though.

Arduously climbing the stairs, he went into the bathroom to retrieve his first aid kit. While he doctored himself, he thought about his next move. The Cabal had taken the key. He could form a small army to get it back by force. But he'd been through so much fighting recently.

It had only been a few months since the slaughter by demons in Sumner, Washington. It had taken him and Ivy hours to bury their friends and burn the rest of the dead. He didn't want to go through that again. And it would be a bloodbath if he went after the Cabal, he had no doubt in his mind.

He washed the wound, poured antiseptic onto it, biting on his lip the whole time. It stung like a thousand bees. He wrapped it tight, then went back down the stairs to his ruined living room. The goblin had done a thorough job of wrecking everything he had. Which, by some standards, wasn't much. His lifestyle didn't really permit the luxuries of living a normal, comfortable life.

Usually on the move, Quinn had only just set up shop in this small starter home, basically for cover. It wasn't as if he worked nine to five at an office. No, he hunted demons. That was his vocation, his life. He'd been born into it.

As far as the people he bought the home from knew, his name was Quinton Sterling, and he was a divorced small-business owner. They'd been more than happy with his story since he paid cash for the place they couldn't afford anymore.

The money came from the other jobs he did. Jobs he wasn't necessarily proud of. Demon hunting wasn't exactly lucrative. He'd pulled a few cons over the years, something he'd learned from his dad. It was a dishonest way to bankroll a lifesaving job of hunting down and destroying demons. Quinn didn't ponder the ethics of it too much.

Righting the overturned sofa, he shoved the ruined cushions back on and sat. He had to think. He had to figure out what to do.

Rubbing his good hand over his face, he sighed. Ultimately, he knew what had to be done next, but he just didn't want to do it. It would be way too complicated and messy. Two things he hated.

If the Cabal had the key, that meant they were going after the chest that contained the book that could unleash hell on Earth. There was only one choice here and that was to find the chest first. Find it and protect it.

Sighing, he leaned his head on the back of the sofa. Maybe there was another way. There had to be. To do what he needed—to uncover where the chest was hidden—would almost be too much to bear. He wasn't sure he could see *her* again.

Quinn found his cell phone on the floor. He picked it up and dialed a familiar number. He glanced at the wall clock. It was only six in the morning. It rang only four times before being answered.

"You do know what time it is?"

He smiled. "Yup, I know, Q. I need to talk."

There came a long, drawn-out sigh. "Fine. Meet me at my office in an hour."

Quinn stood and headed upstairs to get dressed. It was going to be one long, hellish day.

One hour later he stood in the office doorway of Quianna Lang, one of the youngest professors on staff at the San Francisco State University and resident mythologist to the university. But he knew her talents and knowledge lay in demonology. She possessed more knowledge about demons and demon lore than anyone he knew.

She barely looked up from whatever she was reading on her old mahogany desk when he entered. "Sit."

He came all the way in and slid onto one of

the leather chairs situated in front of her big wooden desk.

She finished reading, slammed the book closed and looked up at him. "Okay, so what's going on? How much trouble are you in?"

"Why does something have to be going on?"

She smirked. "Because you're here. The only time you demon hunters come here is when the shit has hit the fan. First Ronan and your sister, and now you. Something major is happening, I suspect."

He sighed, then met her gaze. "The key is gone. Stolen by the Cabal."

Quianna bolted out of her chair and came around the desk. She was a compact woman, short and petite, but she possessed more fire in her pinkie than most people did in their whole bodies. She pinned him to the seat with her intense, determined gaze.

"How?"

"Richter Collins is how. And he had a goblin with him."

She shook her head. "I thought that once Reginald died, the Cabal would fall. I guess I was wrong."

"I should've been more diligent in hiding the key. I had been planning to move it…"

"Well, what's done is done. Now, what are we going to do about it?"

"That's why I came. I thought if anyone would know what to do, it would be you."

She sat on the edge of her desk. "You have to find the chest. You have to get it before they do."

He groaned. "I was hoping there was another way."

"There isn't. If they have the key, they will be going for the chest. That's just logical."

Quinn leaned forward and put his head in his hands. He had been hoping for another answer. Another way to solve the problem.

"I take it you know where it is?" She eyed him curiously.

He shook his head. "Not where. But I know someone who knows."

"By the look on your face, I'd say this some-one is pretty bad."

"You could say that."

She nudged him with her foot. "Well, man up, Quinn. Whatever you have to do, you better do it. This isn't some small problem. We're talk-ing end of days stuff, here. If the Cabal finds that chest and uses that book, it won't matter who this person is, because we'll all be dead."

"When I find the chest and the book, what do I do with them?"

"Bring the book to me. I know a place where even demons fear to tread. I can keep it safe there."

Quinn left Quianna's office with a deep sinking feeling in his gut. It almost made him sick to think about what he had to do to find the chest. But the powerhouse professor had been right, he had to man up and do what needed to be done. No one else was going to do it. He had been entrusted with the key and he had lost it. It had been his responsibility. Now finding the chest was his as well. He was the only one on Earth who could do it. He just had a pit stop to make first.

The new age store located downtown looked like any other crystal and tarot shop. Mary, the proprietor, doled out spiritual wisdom and metaphysical prophecy to every patron that passed through her doors. But when Quinn walked in, she frowned deeply and shook her head.

"I was having a good day," she said.

"Hey, Mary, how's business?"

"On the light side." She moved her hefty frame around the counter to stand in front of him. The beads on her wrists clicked when she moved. The scent of patchouli and lavender wafted to his nose. "But I take it, since you're here, that's going to change."

"I need some supplies."

She sighed heavily, as though she was going to deny him, but she swept her arm toward the back curtain. She never said no; she just liked to put on the drama. She knew he was one of her best customers. He and the Crimson Hall Cabal.

"Come on, then."

Quinn followed her into the back where she kept her stores of "other" types of metaphysical supplies. The type reserved for those who dabbled in the darker side of the magical arts.

"What do you need?"

Quinn examined the shelves of bottles and tins. "Goofer dust, asafoetida, horehound, another blessed chalk stick and some yarrow."

Mary narrowed her eyes at him. "Who are you calling?"

He shrugged. "Don't know what you're talking about."

"The stuff you're asking for, Quinn, is for

calling forth a powerful demon and keeping it in line. Who is it?"

"It doesn't matter. Do you have the stuff or not?" He pulled out a wad of cash from his pocket.

She nodded and went to the shelves to start pulling down jars. "I have everything you need." She stacked it all on the table. She sighed. "Between you and the Cabal, I'm surprised demons aren't running amok on this plane."

Quinn opened his leather satchel and shoved the ingredients inside. He peeled off money and handed it to her.

Mary slid it into the pocket of her flowered housedress but pinned him with a hard glare. "Be careful, Quinn. You're playing with fire."

He nodded. "I know. But it has to be done." Closing his bag, he hefted it onto his shoulder and left the store, his heart as heavy as the bag he carried.

When he got home, he went straight down to the basement to prepare. Using his new blessed chalk he drew a large pentagram on the cement floor, inscribing it with familiar symbols. Symbols he'd been using his whole life as an exorcist and demon hunter. He left two open triangles in the pentagram. This was where he would put the two sigils that would call the demon he needed. They'd been burned into his memory. But for different reasons.

He chalked them in. Around the pentagram he sifted a thick line of goofer dust. It was a protective circle. The demon couldn't cross it if Quinn didn't want it to. And until he got a binding agreement, he didn't plan on letting the demon go anywhere.

Once that was done, Quinn set everything aside, lit seven white candles and started the ritual.

In Latin, he spoke the words to invoke the spell, then he called the demon using its real name. The one that gave him power over it.

"I call you, Daeva, Seductress of Shadows."

At first nothing happened, and Quinn wondered if he'd mistakenly written the symbols backward or upside down. But then a slight breeze blew through the basement. None of the windows were open. Then came the smell. The delectable scent of cinnamon. He tried not to inhale it. But it was difficult not to. Cinnamon had always been one of his favorite smells. It made his gut clench with the memories it brought.

Three popping sounds echoed in the room. Like fingers snapping.

Then it appeared.

Dressed in tight black pants, black leather knee-high boots and a sapphire-blue blouse that accentuated full, firm breasts, the demon smiled at him, and he couldn't suppress the shiver that raced down his back.

"Hello, lover."

Chapter 5

"You look surprised to see *me*, Quinn." Tilting her head, she looked him up and down. "Oh, that's right. You never did get to see me in my preferred form. You were so quick to get rid of me. Never gave me a chance to introduce myself properly."

It had been three years since Daeva had seen Quinn Strom. And she had to admit that he looked as dangerous and delicious as ever. His inner darkness called to her like a moth to a flame. But she couldn't let him see that. She couldn't let him have the upper hand here. She'd never give it to him again.

"How's my favorite exorcist?"

"I didn't call you to have a trite and pointless conversation."

"No? Too bad. That's definitely one thing I missed about you."

She saw him bristle and grinned. Score one for Daeva.

Quinn had always prided himself on his ability to speak on all kinds of subjects. On several occasions, he'd bored her to tears. But she'd listened to him attentively. That was what a person did when they were in love.

Love. Ha. Quinn Strom knew nothing about the emotion. If he had, he'd never have done what he did to her.

But, alas, she obviously was not here to discuss the past. Quinn had something dire to talk to her about, or he would never have called her forth. Never. She knew him well enough to know that he held a grudge the way a miser held money.

"So, to what do I owe this utmost pleasure of seeing your handsome face again?" Although she had her suspicions that it had everything to do with her twelve-hour torture session and Klaven's questions.

Thankfully, that had ended without Daeva revealing much of anything—nothing important anyway. He'd poked and prodded at her until he'd gotten bored. And her restorative powers made it look like she'd barely been bruised. Although the truth was it had taken a lot out of her and she was feeling its effects.

"I need information."

"I gathered that. On what?"

"The Chest of Sorrows."

And there it was. She'd known it deep down, the moment she'd heard that the little goblin Loir had gone topside for a key. Loir had confirmed it herself when she snuck into Daeva's chambers as she healed from her torture session to warn her. Sorcerers used goblins for some of their work. She assumed it was one of the cabals that had stolen the key from the great Quinn Strom. She was surprised he was still alive.

"What do you want to know that you don't already?" she asked.

He paced nervously in front of the pentagram. Usually he paced when he wasn't quite confident in what he was doing or the decisions he was making. "Where is it?"

She laughed. "Are you kidding? Do you really think I'm going to tell you that?"

"Yes, I do." He gave her a hard stare.

She'd always loved his gray-green eyes. They were so intense. Always searching for something. At one time, he'd look at her with those eyes and she'd see the desire in them and succumb to it. She'd surrender to him without a second thought.

Now, he looked at her as if she was the worst thing he'd ever seen. She supposed betrayal did that to a person.

"What are you going to do, Quinn, if I don't tell you?" She arched an eyebrow and ran a finger along her lips. "Torture it out of me?"

"I might."

"You're a bastard, true. But I don't think you have it in you to do that to me."

"Maybe I've changed in the last three years."

She met his gaze, looking for something of the old Quinn. The man she'd loved, who had loved her. After a few seconds, she wasn't sure he was still in there. "Oh, I suspect you have. But you still have those interesting morals.

Those you will never let go of, I am sure. I fell victim to them, as I recall, once upon a time."

He sighed and rubbed a hand over his haggard face. It was obvious he hadn't slept in a while. He looked harder, sadder. As though he held the world on his shoulders. She supposed he did, in a way, considering that he'd been the key keeper and now no doubt felt responsible for finding the chest and keeping it safe.

Quinn had always been a crusader. It was one of the things she'd loved about him. And that had also been the thing that had killed their relationship in the end. His single-minded sense of justice.

He could never see the shades of gray in between those morals of his.

Gray had always been her favorite color.

"I called you, Daeva, thinking there was some sort of good person inside you. A person who would do the right thing."

She laughed again. "The right thing? Huh. And what exactly is that, Quinn?"

He stared at her and she stared back. It was the showdown they'd never had when she'd possessed the body of the woman he'd fallen in love with. The woman she'd been, mind, body and soul for ten years. Seven years before she'd even met Quinn and fallen for him.

At first when she'd confessed her secret about being a demon, he hadn't truly believed her. He'd thought she was pulling a really bad prank on him. He'd asked her a lot of questions to prove it. Daeva had told him things only a demon would know, and she'd also told him about burying the Chest of Sorrows over a hundred years ago. It was then that he had truly believed. And it was as if a switch had been flicked on. He'd gone into demon hunter mode.

He'd bound her to a chair, drawn a pentagram around her, sprayed her with holy water and sent her screaming back to hell. How he'd dealt with Rachel's comatose body, she could only imagine. Maybe the real woman had woken up.

Daeva had never gotten a chance to say goodbye to anything that had mattered to her. The friends she'd made, family members who had loved her like their own, coworkers she'd grown accustomed to. She hadn't had a chance to say goodbye to the life she'd made. She hadn't been able to say goodbye to Quinn the way she wanted to.

When he had her tied in that chair, he'd acted

as if they hadn't spent three wonderful years together. That they hadn't just spent the entire day
before in bed, making love and talking about
their future. He'd pretended that he hadn't just
told her that he loved her more than anything in
the world. She remembered the tears, though,
and the way he'd looked at her through them.

He dropped his gaze. "Are you going to tell
me or not?"

She tapped a finger against her lips. "Hmm,
since you asked so nicely, I think not."

"I guess I was kidding myself, thinking a
demon would even consider doing the right
thing."

"Yeah, maybe you were. You seem to do that
a lot."

He glared at her, then went to the wall,
grabbed a folding chair and dragged it out to the
middle of the room, in front of the pentagram.
He unfolded it and sat. "I can sit here all night."

She smirked at him, then settled onto the hard
cement floor, crossing her legs. "So can I."

For the next hour, they sat and stared at each
other. Daeva broke her gaze once in a while to
examine her nails. It seemed to piss Quinn off
and that's why she did it. She really didn't think

that her nails were more important than the situation. She just liked to revel in the way the vein at his right temple would throb.

"What happened to your arm?" she asked.

"What do you care?"

"I don't. I'm just being polite."

He held his forearm up and looked at it. "Courtesy of your little goblin friend."

"Loir did that to you?"

He nodded.

"Well, then, you must've deserved it. I'm surprised that she didn't kill you. She's usually very bloodthirsty." Daeva spoke with her tongue in cheek, because Loir was anything but. She was one of the kindest creatures Daeva knew. Unless, of course, she was forced to do something. Then she could be lethal.

"I'm surprised she didn't, as well. She said you would hate it if she killed me."

Daeva examined her nails again. "Hmm, she must have been mistaken. I'm pretty sure I wouldn't have alluded to such a thing."

She had though. In her note. She'd simply written, "Don't kill him."

Another half hour went by. He was as stubborn as she remembered him to be. Maybe more so. She didn't remember the stern wrinkles in his brow, the way it was now. That was new. But she had a feeling it had something to do with her. She'd put those lines of pain there.

She sighed. "Are we seriously going to sit here all night?"

"Until you help me, yes."

"I never said I wouldn't help you, Quinn, I just can't tell you where the chest is."

"Can't or won't?"

She shrugged. "Whatever makes you feel better."

"Well, that's the only help I need. The location. So if you won't give it to me, then there's nothing to talk about."

She stood and brushed the dirt off her black pants. "Fine. Send me back, then. I have laundry to do."

He looked at her, and she could see the hesitation on his face. He obviously hadn't expected her to call his bluff. He should've known she would. She possessed all the same personality traits she had when she'd been wearing a human birthday suit. She was basically the same, except for a few physical changes.

Sighing, he shook his head. "What's it going to take?"

"I'll help you find the chest, but I want something in return."

"Of course you do," he sneered.

"Play nice or you can forget it. And when the Cabal opens the chest and uses the book, and your world goes to shit, don't complain to me about it." She pointed a finger at him. "Besides, you know as well as I do that it's the nature of my…condition to make a bargain."

"What are your terms?"

"I guide you to where the chest is, you get it, and in return I get to stay topside in a new body forever."

Quinn stood, his chair overturning from the suddenness of his movement. The banging of metal on cement echoed through the basement. "Absolutely not."

"Then send me back, because those are my terms and I won't change them."

He shook his head. "Nope. That's too easy." He turned toward the stairs. "We'll see how cooperative you are after a few more hours in that pentagram." He mounted the stairs.

She watched him leave. When he was at the

top of the stairs he flicked off the light. The room plunged into darkness. Not a big deal for Daeva, though—she could see in the dark. But it was starting to get drafty. Right now she was almost missing the hot stifling air in hell.

"You're a jerk, Quinn Strom."

He slammed the door shut on her words.

Chapter 6

Quinn tried to keep himself busy. Tried to keep his mind occupied. But it was difficult with a demon in his basement. Especially one that smelled like cinnamon and looked like sex on a stick.

She'd been right, her appearance did startle him. When he'd known her, she'd been a lithe blond with an athletic build and a pert little nose. Her name had been Rachel. The demon who had popped into the pentagram was a curvy redhead with stormy gray eyes. She looked very different from the woman he'd loved, but something about her was still the same. The fluid way she moved, the tilt of her head as she regarded him. If he had passed her on the street, he suspected he would've recognized her.

The thought was completely unnerving. He didn't want to recognize the woman from three years ago in the demon he'd just called. He wanted them to be two distinct entities, but deep down he knew that they weren't. They were like two sides of one complicated coin. He supposed Daeva had always been a part of Rachel, however much he wanted to deny it.

By the third hour, after straightening up everything the goblin had ruined, Quinn ended up in the kitchen to make dinner. He flung open the refrigerator and started pulling out various ingredients. He grabbed a pot and a pan, and tossed in this and that, frying and boiling, anything to occupy his thoughts. In the end, he had made spaghetti Bolognese. It had been one of Rachel's favorite meals. And he'd made enough for two.

"Damn it," he mumbled under his breath.

He stared at the food, unsure of exactly what to do. He could make himself a plate and put the rest in containers for leftovers. Or he could fix another plate and take it down to his captive. Demons didn't derive any nutrition from food, but he knew they reveled in all mortal pleasures. Like food, and drink, and sex.

Resigned, Quinn grabbed two plates from the cupboard and put spaghetti onto both. Picking up one plate, he got a fork and took it down to the basement.

He flicked on the lights. As if weighted down with leaden feet, he descended the stairs. When he reached the bottom, he saw Daeva sitting cross-legged in the middle of the pentagram with her eyes closed. It looked as if she was meditating.

"Oh, my, is that spaghetti Bolognese I smell?" Her eyelids slowly fluttered open.

He gestured with the plate. "I wasn't sure if you were hungry or not."

She studied him for a moment, then nodded. "I am."

Nearing the pentagram, he reached across the lines and handed her the food. She took it from him and set it in her lap. She picked up the fork, spun it in the noodles, then put it in her mouth. She grinned around the mouthful. When she was done chewing, she looked up at him.

"Good Lord, that is so good." She twirled her fork in it again. "I've instructed the goblins on how to prepare it properly, but they never get it right. It always tastes so sour. Must be the water in hell. Can't seem to get that sulfur flavor out, no matter how long you boil it."

He watched her eat, a sense of pride and satisfaction filling his gut. He'd always loved that Rachel had enjoyed his cooking. There had been many nights when they'd spent hours in the kitchen together preparing a meal, talking, laughing, eating. The thought now made him sad. And angry. Angry that those memories were tarnished by her true existence. By Daeva's existence.

"Where's yours?" she asked.

"Upstairs."

"Didn't want to eat with the demon?"

"Something like that."

She shrugged. "Suit yourself." She shoveled more of the spaghetti into her mouth.

"I don't want to play this game anymore."

She set her fork down and regarded him. "Then don't."

"I can't in good conscience give you what you're asking for."

"Why not?"

"I can't let you possess someone, Daeva. Take over her life like that. You have no idea what I had to deal with after you left Rachel's body."

"Did she die?" Something about asking that made her face pale. She actually looked extremely concerned.

"No, she woke up and was hysterical. She had no idea what she was doing there or who I was."

"What did you do with her?"

"I took her to her parents' house and told them she fell and hit her head and didn't remember me." He rubbed at his face, hating to have to relive it. "They took her to the hospital and ran tests on her. I slowly removed myself from her life. Her parents hated me for it."

She eyed him intensely for a moment. He thought maybe she was going to apologize to him, but then she sighed, and leaned back onto her hands. "You can have the veto over the body I possess."

"In what way?"

"When the time comes, after you have the chest in your hands, I will pick a body and if you disagree, you can veto me."

Quinn looked at her, mulling over her words,

trying to find the catch, the loophole. There were always loopholes in demon deals. But in every scenario he conjured in his mind, he couldn't find a way she could deceive him. Ultimately, in the end, he could stop her from possessing anyone. He just had to continually say no.

"Agreed."

"Excellent." She picked up her plate. "Just let me finish this, then we can hammer out the details." She started to eat again.

Slightly off balance, Quinn mounted the stairs to head back to the kitchen to eat his dinner. All the way there, he was sure that she'd gotten the upper hand on him. She was much too calm and reserved about the whole thing. But, as he ate his spaghetti, he couldn't figure out why.

Once he was finished eating, he returned to the basement with his book of Latin rites. Daeva was standing, her empty plate right on the edge of the pentagram. She must've pushed it as far as she could without crossing the lines.

"Okay. You ready?" she asked.

"No, but I guess at this juncture I don't have a choice."

She smiled. "You always have a choice Quinn. You're human. You've got free will."

He didn't say anything else on the subject. He didn't feel like having an ethical or theological discussion with a demon right now. "Once I release you from the pentagram, will you have powers?"

She nodded. "Although I'll be losing some because of the bargain we've made. I won't be able to zip through the ether with a snap of my fingers. For all intents and purposes I will be human. Well, a human with super strength and other goodies. Not sure what, though. Need to test them out."

Quinn was nervous. He'd never released a demon from a bound pentagram before. That was how his father had died. On the job, after releasing a demon he thought he could trust. *Demon* and *trust* were two words that didn't go together.

He'd dealt with demons when they'd been bound inside a pentagram and when they'd been possessing someone. But he couldn't think of another way to find the chest. He knew that Daeva, alone, had hidden it a hundred years ago. If he didn't bind her with an agreement, he was certain someone else would. Like Richter Collins of the Crimson Hall Cabal. Once the sorcerer found out that the demon was the only one with that knowledge, he'd be looking to make a deal with her. And he wouldn't bother with ethics.

Quinn opened the book to the right page and, holding his hand out toward the pentagram, began speaking the Latin words of the ritual.

When he was done, he took his ceremonial dagger and cupped it in his hand, slicing his palm open. Blood dripping onto the cement floor, he held his hand out to Daeva.

"Now yours."

Palm up, she offered her hand to him. He quickly drew the blade across her skin. Instantly, blood welled to the top.

"Until the bargain is complete, Daeva, Seductress of Shadows, you are bound to the Earth and to me."

They shook hands, their blood mixing, the power of the bargain sealing them together. He could feel the potency of it sizzling the hair on his arms.

Quinn pulled his hand away first and quickly

wrapped it with gauze. Daeva squeezed her hand tight, but blood dripped from the corners.

"You aren't going to heal as fast," he offered. "Give me your hand."

Daeva stepped out of the pentagram to stand beside him. She looked around, seemingly surprised to find herself unbound by the blessed lines. She smiled and took in a deep breath. "Finally."

He saw the extreme relief on her face and he wondered if this was her first time being free. Well, not completely free—she was bound to him, which meant no matter where she went he could find her or compel her to return to his side. She was also free from exorcism. Which meant no one could send her back to hell. Except for him, that was.

"You're bleeding all over the place. Give me your damn hand."

She held her hand out to him. As quick as he could, he cleaned her up and wrapped her wound.

She tested it by clenching and unclenching her fist, then nodded. "Thanks."

As he'd doctored her hand, he'd noticed a few scars on her arm. They'd looked fresh and sore. He wondered what they were from but didn't want to ask. He didn't want to seem as if he cared.

"Okay, before we go on this little adventure, we need to set some rules."

Smirking, she shook her head. "You and your rules."

"I just want to make sure I don't end up with a knife in my back and you on the run."

She pinned him with her gaze. He had to suppress a shiver. "Despite everything, I can't believe you'd even think I would do that to you."

Her words gave him a slight pause. He had to keep chanting in his mind, *she's a demon, she's a demon, and not the woman I fell in love with.* But her gaze was fierce and hard and serious. As if he'd actually hurt her feelings by even suggesting she would betray him like that.

"Wouldn't you?" He met her gaze right on. He wasn't about to back down, to cower before her.

She took a step away from him, then licking her lips, she glanced up the stairs. "I'm earthbound to you, Quinn. I couldn't run even if I wanted to. And for the other part, quit being a dick and maybe I won't consider it."

He laughed at that. He couldn't help it. In the past, the insult had been one of Rachel's favorite things to call him when he was being difficult. It had always made him laugh when she said it.

Surprised, she looked at him and smiled. "Oh, so there is a human being in there somewhere."

"Yeah, deeply buried."

"I knew it."

His laughter died down and he set his shoulders straight. They had to get to work. He suspected the Cabal would be on his ass soon. Once they found out that Daeva had been called out of hell, and by whom, they would have little time.

"So, where are we going?"

"Well, we'll need a car, lots of gas and supplies."

"Where are we going, Daeva?"

She sighed. "Look, I can't tell you that. It's for your own safety. If you're captured and questioned, you can't give them the location."

"And I won't be able to ditch you, either."

She ran her tongue over her top lip. "There is that, too."

He nodded, resigned to having to do it her way for a while. He just wanted to find the

chest. If he had to follow her directions he'd
do it. "Fine."

"Great. Now that that's solved. I need to clean
up." She pushed past him to go up the stairs.
"Do you have any bubble bath?"

Chapter 7

"No, I don't have any damn bubble bath," Quinn growled at her as he mounted the stairs behind her.

From the stairs she came out into the kitchen. It was small and cozy with a compact island in the middle. The scent of the sauce he'd made for the spaghetti still clung to the air.

She looked left then right. "Where's your bathroom?"

"Upstairs."

She moved through the kitchen and into

the living room. She took in the destruction. "Maid's day off?"

"Courtesy of your goblin friend, again, and the Cabal."

She didn't comment as she strode across the room and up the staircase, Quinn right on her heels.

"We don't have time for your frivolous needs, Daeva. We should be on the move."

She found the bathroom, but turned toward him before entering. "Look, I've spent the last few years in a stinking cesspool of misery and mayhem, thanks to you no less. I'm taking time to wash off the smell."

"Well, since I'm the one that called you forth and released you, I think that makes me in charge."

She smiled at him, putting a hand on one hip. "I may be bound to you, honey, but you don't command me. There's a huge difference, you know?"

He frowned. "I know the difference."

"No, I don't think you do." She took a step back into the bathroom, then slammed the door shut on Quinn's next protestation. With a satisfied sigh, she locked the door.

"Daeva, we don't have time for this crap."

"Sure we do, lover. While I bathe this beautiful body of mine why don't you get what you need ready. Make sure you pack an extra pair of shorts, it's going to be a long trip."

She heard his exasperated sigh, and it tickled her inside. Let him suffer for a while. Fair was fair. Besides, she really did want to wash off the stench of sulfur she was sure still clung to her skin and clothes.

Plus, it would give her a bit of a reprieve from the sensations surging through her at seeing Quinn again. She didn't think it would be this hard to be near him, with his masculine scent tantalizing her senses. The urge to touch him warred with the desire to slug him in his pointy nose.

Maybe she was being silly by demanding a bath when obviously there was a level of danger hovering over everything. But she found she couldn't just jump in as Quinn's traveling partner, however forced it was. It was a bit too much too soon. She'd just returned from three years in hell, sent there by the man beyond the door. She needed a little time to decompress her anger. Anger that she was surprised she still harbored. Seeing him face-to-face manifested that bitterness.

Daeva turned on the sink tap and splashed cold water on her face. She looked up into the mirror at herself. It was strange to be topside in her true form, well, almost true form. She was minus the fangs and glowy-type skin. She'd gotten so used to seeing Rachel's face in the mirror that her real appearance sometimes startled her. She could just imagine what it was doing to Quinn. Maybe she should give him a break. This was probably just as difficult for him as it was for her. She gave him credit though, for swallowing his enormous pride and calling her. Asking a demon for help must've really pricked him in the ass.

Straightening, she patted her face dry with the hand towel. She opened the door. She supposed she'd give him that break. Although his suffering was sweet, she did possess a heart and conscience somewhere deep inside.

He was there leaning against the wall when she stepped out.

"I thought you needed a bath?"

She shrugged. "Nah, I just needed a minute

to adjust to topside. It's a bit unstable up here. The Earth's always moving."

He stared at her as though he didn't know whether to believe her or not. He opened his mouth to respond but she grabbed his arm and yanked him to her.

His eyes widened when she leaned into his ear. "We have company."

"Are you sure?" Quinn whispered.

She nodded. "Sounds like three or four men. Two at the front, one or two at the back."

"Damn it." He cursed a few more times. "Must be the Cabal. They're earlier than I thought."

"I could go blast them."

He shook his head. "No. No blasting until we absolutely need to." He moved to the stairs. "We have to get back to the basement."

She followed him, close behind. "Won't we be trapping ourselves?"

He shook his head. "Trust me. I'm always prepared."

They made it back downstairs without incident. He rushed to one wall, slid his hands along the wallboard until he found a groove. He dug his fingers into it and pulled a piece off. Behind it were two duffel bags.

He grabbed them both, tossing one to her, then he pointed to the small window. "We'll go out that way. I have a car parked about five blocks away for emergencies."

She watched him pull the metal bars from the opening. Obviously they were there only for show. He tossed his bag through then dragged a chair over and set it underneath.

"You first."

Although she was better equipped to stay behind and deal with the Cabal if they rushed down the stairs, she didn't argue with him. Stepping up onto the chair, she pushed her bag out then reached through the window, grabbed hold of a tree root that was pushing through the grass and pulled herself up. Kicking her legs, she managed to wriggle her way out the small opening.

Once on her feet, she reached down and helped pull Quinn through. It proved a little harder for him to squeeze out the window opening. He was much thicker than she was.

They peered around for any sign of sorcerers

lurking. She couldn't see anything, even with her night vision. "We're clear," she told him.

"Okay. We run east about five blocks. There is a dark blue sedan parked on the right side. Keys are hidden on the right front wheel under the fender."

"Got it."

Quinn draped a bag handle around each shoulder, then took off. Daeva did the same and was right behind him. She'd run barely a block before she felt the first zing of magic behind her. She glanced over her shoulder just as a green bolt of energy slammed into the azalea bush she'd just passed.

"They're on us!" she shouted to Quinn who was maybe three feet in front of her. "You get to the car. I'll slow them down."

She didn't wait for him to respond. She stopped running and turned, already conjuring a ball of dark fire in her right palm. As a demon on this plane, she should have possessed many powers. Telekinesis, manipulation of elements—especially fire—moving through shadows. But she wasn't sure which ones would work now that she was Quinn bound.

Her hands heated quickly, so she assumed her

firepower was still intact. Once she had a good-sized fiery globe in her hand, she launched it at the two sorcerers running down the street toward her. The ball hit the pavement in front of them, sending up sparks, and a wall of flame.

It wouldn't last long, so she hoped Quinn had made it to the vehicle. Before the flames could go out, she made another ball in her left hand. It wasn't nearly as big or powerful, but it would have to do. She had always been right-handed.

But before she could release it, a bolt of magic clipped her in the shoulder, and she dropped the sphere of fire. The moment it hit the sidewalk, it exploded in an array of sparks and flames leaped at her. She dived to the right and fell onto her side on the grass before her pants started to burn.

She looked up just as two other sorcerers advanced on her, their hands glowing green with power. Rolling, she gained her feet and started to run, but they were right on her ass. Sudden jolts of searing pain rushed up her back. The impact of their magic pushed her forward and she stumbled again, falling to her knees.

She couldn't believe the pain surging over her body. She'd never felt anything like that before.

Obviously she was more fragile topside than she was in hell. The binding must've made her human like.

A kick in the back of her head sent her face down to the cement. She tried to push up, but one of the men pressed her down with his boot on her back.

"We got the demon bitch," one of the men called.

"There's no need for name-calling." Daeva pushed up with all her strength, sweeping her leg at the man. She knocked over the sorcerer standing on her.

Once he was down, she stumbled to her feet. But the other one was there, grabbing her by the back of the head.

"Where do you think you're going?"

In the distance, she could see a vehicle bearing down on them. Twisting around, she punched the goon in the sternum and sent him sprawling backward. Fortunately he let go of her hair.

She bolted to the right just as Quinn barreled the car right into the sorcerer. He rolled over the hood, then off the car to land in a heap on the road.

Daeva opened the back door and dived into the car. Quinn backed it up, tires squealing, did a four-point turn and raced away from the magical goon squad.

A couple of bursts of green magic hit the back of the car. One busted a taillight, but it was nothing that would stop the vehicle. Tires squealed as Quinn turned the car around a corner to the main road, then finally out of the neighborhood and onto a major highway.

Daeva lay on her stomach in the backseat, gaining her breath and trying to gauge her injuries. Which was something new. She remembered being hurt when she had possessed a body. She'd felt pain before, but it had been buffered in a way. This was excruciatingly different. She felt the burn all the way to her bones.

"Are you okay?" Quinn asked.

"I'll live." She sat up, careful of her shoulder and her head. She had a headache that thumped all over her skull and neck.

He looked at her in the rearview mirror. "Are you injured?"

"A little. Nothing that won't heal."

He nodded, and it looked as if he wanted to say more, but he didn't, just glanced down at the car controls and turned up the heat. "So, now that we're out, where are we going?"

"North."

"To?"

"Just drive north for now."

"I need to know, Daeva."

She sighed. "Get us to the Canadian border, then I'll let you know."

"Got a passport? You're going to need it to get over."

She smiled, then rested her head on the seat. "I'll figure something out."

"Which border crossing?"

"Through Washington. Easier to cross." She shut her eyes, blocking out the pain, the streetlights and Quinn. For now, she needed to think about how she was going to get out of their arrangement and be able to stay topside. Because she knew deep down that he would look for some way to screw her over.

Chapter 8

Quinn watched Daeva in the rearview mirror as he drove out of the city. She had her eyes closed, and she looked as though she was asleep. He'd be surprised if she was. As far as he knew, demons didn't need sleep. They recharged in other ways.

Wrath demons gained strength from anger, sloth demons from being lazy asses, and lust demons, of which he was sure she was one, got it from sex or sexual energy. She was certainly built like a lust demon. Curvy, sexy, intoxicat-

ing, really. He found it difficult to look at her
and not think of sex.

He reached over to the controls and turned
down the heat. He was already sweating; he
didn't need to make it worse. He flipped the
vent toward his face and blasted it with cool
fresh air. This was going to be one long journey.

"I'm not one, you know."

He glanced in the mirror and saw that Daeva's eyes were open. "Excuse me?

"A lust demon. I'm not one. Not really." She
shrugged. "Well, I definitely have ancestors in
that realm, but I'm not full blooded."

"I don't know why you're telling me this." He
licked his lips feeling uncomfortable.

"Yes, you do. Don't be coy."

He met her piercing gaze in the mirror. "It's
not polite to read people's minds."

She smiled then, and it lit up her face. "I
wasn't reading your mind. It was your...ah,
other parts I was getting information from."

Quinn grunted, then pulled the car off the
road and into a busy roadside gas station and
diner. "We should dump this car and get a new
one. The Cabal saw this one. They might be
tracking us."

There were roughly twenty vehicles in the parking lot. He pulled along the side of the station, where there were another five. These likely belonged to the staff. They'd take one of these because it would likely be a longer delay until the vehicle was noticed as missing. Hopefully they'd be long gone and have switched vehicles again farther along the road in one of the small towns.

Quinn parked the car, then turned in the seat to look at Daeva. He took in her black leggings, noticing the small burn holes and the frays in her blouse. "You need to change clothes. You look too conspicuous."

She smirked. "I didn't really pack an extra set of clothes."

"I have a pair of jeans and a T-shirt in one of the bags."

She titled her head to look at him. Something sad filled her eyes. "Just like old times, hey?"

He stared at her, anger, sorrow and regret filling him to the brim. He had to fight two urges, one to punch his fist into the seat and the other to breach the distance between them and take her mouth with his. He hated her for making him feel both.

"It's not old times. The woman who wore my T-shirt to bed is not here anymore. You killed her."

"No. You did when you exorcised me back to hell."

He'd had enough. He jumped out of the car, grabbing the bag off the front seat. Angrily, he pulled open the back door. "Get out."

She did.

He shoved the bag into her arms. "The clothes are in here. I suggest you get changed quickly. I'm leaving in ten minutes."

For a minute, it looked as if she might cry. He could see the liquid in her steely eyes. Quinn tensed up, guilt churning in his gut. But when he looked again, her face was hard and icy again, like a granite statue.

"Oh, I doubt that, Quinn. You don't even know where you're going." Hooking the bag over her shoulder, she sashayed into the gas station as if she hadn't a care in the world.

Once she was gone, he surveyed the choice of vehicles. There were three trucks and two sedans. Making sure no one was around, he discreetly tried the doors on the first sedan. All locked. The second sedan wasn't as secure. The right back door was unlocked.

He slid in, jumped into the front and busted the ignition panel. There were several wires peeking out, but he knew which ones to cut and tie together. He'd hot-wired many vehicles in the past. It was part of the transient demon-hunting lifestyle. The trick was something his dad had taught him years ago.

He tapped two stripped wires together and the engine jumped to life. Quinn tied them off, then opened the door and slid out. He had to re-trieve the other bag from his car. Then they'd be ready to go.

After he got his other bag, he walked back to the sedan. That's when he saw Daeva com-ing toward him. She'd changed clothes as he re-quested. He'd been sure it would make her less sexy, less of a standout, more like the average girl next door. But seeing her with his T-shirt on, pulled tight across her breasts, his jeans tight around her hips and with her long hair pulled back from her face into a high ponytail made his heart skip a few beats and his gut tighten.

She looked like the woman he remembered loving years ago. She'd often wear her hair pulled back, especially on the weekends. It was something he'd always found attractive about her, because her face was striking, electric, and it had always lit up when she'd seen him.

Like now.

He rubbed a hand over his stomach. Damn, she was potent. It was like getting hit in the gut by a battering ram. But it had to be her demon powers working their mojo on him. It had to be. Because the alternative made every part of him hum with nervous energy.

"What?" she asked as she neared him. "You look like you've seen a ghost."

He scanned her, spotting a rather long scar on her forearm. He gestured to it. "How did you get that? I thought demons can regenerate."

She lifted her arm and regarded at it. "Yeah, well, let's just say it's a reminder of why I'm here and what I need to do."

"That's pretty vague."

"Yes, it is."

He shook his head. "Fine. Forget I cared." He pulled open the car door. "Let's just go."

She rounded the car, opened the back door and dumped the bag, then opened the passenger door and slid in. After buckling up, she tossed him a granola bar. "Thought you might be hungry."

He picked it up and looked at it. "You didn't steal it, did you?"

She unwrapped the one she had in her hand and took a bite. "Nah. I found a ten-dollar bill in your jeans pocket."

He laughed then. He couldn't help himself. He tore off the wrapper and took a healthy bite. "Thanks."

"You're most welcome." She smiled around the next bite in her mouth.

He put the car into drive, backed up out of the parking stall and drove it out onto the road.

After about ten minutes of Quinn fiddling with the heat controls, seat adjustments and the radio, Daeva turned it off. "Are we going to talk about it?"

"Talk about what?"

"You know what."

He sighed, and ran a hand over his face. He was tired. There was nothing more that he wanted right now than to lie down and sleep for a few hours. To turn the world off for just a little while. But Daeva wasn't giving him that time.

"Why? What difference does it make?"

"If we have to work together for the next few days, I think we should clear the air."

"I'd rather not, okay?" He flipped on the radio again.

She shut it off. "Why? It's been years, let's just talk about it."

"Because it still hurts, damn it!" He slammed his fist against the steering wheel.

She was silent, but he could feel her gaze on him. He didn't want her to look at him, to see the hurt on his face. He'd been sure he'd gotten over it, gotten over her. The way his heart throbbed and his gut churned told him he wasn't over anything.

"I'm sorry, Quinn."

He glanced at her. There was a liquid shimmer in her eyes. A shimmer he wanted to convince himself couldn't possibly exist. That she was incapable of such emotion.

"You never gave me a chance to explain. To tell you how it happened. How I came to be inside Rachel and how I fell for you."

He shook his head. "I don't want to hear it."

She reached across the seat and settled her hand on top of his on the steering wheel. "You need to hear it. And I need to say it."

He was about to respond when bright lights flashed on behind the car. Headlights bore down on them. Quinn could hear the roar of an engine.

"Shit! They found us."

Daeva swirled in the seat to look out the rear window. "How did they track us?"

He shook his head. "I don't know, but hang on to something."

Daeva gripped the door handle and the dash as he stepped on the gas and veered around a truck on the road in front of them. The vehicle behind them followed closely. It was going to take more than going faster to shake them.

"I can blast them."

Quinn glanced over at Daeva. Her right hand was starting to glow red. "Wait. Wait until we're off the main road. I'm going to take the next turnoff."

Racing at seventy, it was hard to see the exit. But the second Quinn spied it he yanked the wheel to the right and they were skidding sideways to take the road. The car felt as if it was going to tip, but he had control. He'd done his fair share of fancy driving in the past. He knew how to handle a car.

Once they were righted, he pressed on the

gas. They needed to find a way to hide. He wasn't going to be able to outrun the other vehicle. Not out here in the middle of nowhere without anything to hide behind.

"Look for a place to turn off. Lots of trees would be good," he instructed.

He checked in the rearview mirror for the other vehicle. He saw headlights not far behind them. "Damn it! If we turn they'll see it."

"Turn off the lights."

He gaped at her. "How is that going to help? I'll crash if I can't see."

"I can see in the dark." She unbuckled her seatbelt and started to slide across the seat. "Trust me. Let me drive."

"We can't do this at this speed."

"Slow down a bit, then." She glanced back. "We have some space."

Quinn thought it was crazy, but he couldn't think of another way. Being in the dark would give them the advantage. He braked a little, slowing to fifty. He undid his seatbelt, then lifted up so Daeva could slide in under him.

He felt her foot next to his, and he took it off the gas pedal and pushed himself to the right over top of her. The car veered a bit, but Daeva was down in the seat, hands on the wheel and foot on the pedal before they could go into the ditch.

He settled in the passenger seat and buckled up. "Okay. We're good to go."

She fiddled on the left side of the steering wheel and then the headlights flicked off. She fiddled some more with the wires hanging out and the brake lights blinked off, as well. It was nearly pitch black in front of them. It scared the hell out of him, driving blind, but it looked as though Daeva had it under control. She was focused on the road without any problem.

"Get ready. There's a turnoff ahead on the left. Lots of trees and bushes."

Quinn braced himself against the dash and floor.

Without another warning, Daeva yanked the wheel to the left. He could hear the gravel spitting up behind the tires as they took the corner. Once around, she slowed down a little.

He turned and watched out the back window. After another five seconds, he saw the vehicle speed past. "It worked."

"We should still get off the road." She made

another left turn onto a heavily treed gravel road, then slowed even more.

"Pull it into the ditch."

She did, in a space behind some bushes. She put the car in Park but left it running just in case. "How could they track us? We ditched the car."

He rubbed at his forehead, a headache threatened to come. "Not sure. They do have magical tracking abilities. As far as I know they can't pinpoint an exact position, just an area."

"Yeah, but don't they have to physically touch you or something?"

"Just their magic," he said.

Her eyes went wide as she looked at him. "I think I'm bugged."

"What? How?"

"I got clipped in the shoulder when we were getting out of your place." She hooked her fingers in the hem of the T-shirt and pulled it over her head.

"What are you doing?"

She pointed to the burn on the back of her right shoulder blade. "Look."

He did. At first he saw nothing but the raw and bloody skin, but when he peered at the wound closer, he spied the telltale green glow of magic still pulsating. It was a tracer and it was deep inside Daeva's flesh.

Chapter 9

"It's there, isn't it?"

Quinn nodded grimly. "I'm going to have to dig it out."

"It's going to hurt like hell, isn't it?" The thought of more pain made her stomach roil. She hadn't quite gotten used to the agony of being almost human yet.

He licked his lips, then nodded. "Yeah."

"Then do it quickly."

"Daeva…"

"Look, we are only safe for a little bit, then

they will be following this tracker. You know
it's the only way. So just do it."

Quinn unbuckled the knife on his belt. "Turn
a bit, so I can get at it."

She did, then one of his hands was on her
shoulder and the other had the blade tip braced
against her skin. She sucked in a breath, preparing for the pain that was sure to come. But
Quinn was hesitating.

"What's the holdup? You need to do it."

She looked over her shoulder at him, but he
wasn't focused on her wound. He was looking
farther down her back. And she knew what he
saw there. Long raised welts. Ones a person
could only get from a whip.

"Jesus, Daeva. What happened?"

"It doesn't matter. Just do what you need to
do."

"Who hurt you?"

She sighed, not wanting to talk about it. She
wanted to forget the whole thing ever happened.
But she knew she couldn't, not with the evi-
dence on her skin. "Before you summoned me,
I was…interrogated about you."

"What? Why?"

"Because the demons are looking for the

same thing the Cabal is, or are working with the Cabal. Don't know which. Everyone is looking for the key and the chest."

"You told them where I lived?"

"No." She licked her lips, not wanting to remember the torture. "But after twelve hours of…well, I sure wanted to."

She laughed it off, but she felt no humor in it. This was just one of many reasons she never wanted to go back to hell. She couldn't and stay sane.

"No one should have to go through something like that."

She shrugged. "It's just another day in hell." She saw him cringe at that, maybe feeling a little guilt at having sent her back there. "It's done, so let's move on and get this over with. We don't have much time."

Quinn nodded. Then, gripping her shoulder hard to keep her from flinching, he pressed the tip of the knife to her skin. Without any more hesitation, he slid the blade in, slicing skin and flesh.

The pain ripped through her, but she kept still, knowing he had to dig the tracker out. If she moved, he might cut her unnecessarily. She bit down on her lip as Quinn scraped at her flesh. Sweat popped out on her forehead. It took all she had not to cry out.

Then it was done, and he was wiping his blade clean of her blood.

"It's gone. It dissipated." He set the knife down, then grabbed one of the bags and took out a first aid kit to doctor her up quickly and efficiently.

Once she was bandaged, Daeva pulled his T-shirt back on. The ache in her shoulder was deep, but she'd push through the pain. It could've been worse, she supposed.

"Let's get out of here. They could still be around." She put the car in gear and pulled back out onto the road. The one back wheel spit back gravel, but they got out.

As she drove, making several turns and loops in case they were still being followed, Quinn busied himself by cleaning his knife and re-sorting his medical supplies. She caught him glancing at her every so often. She could tell he had something to say to her.

"Just spit it out," she said.

"What?"

"I can tell you have something on your mind.

You're looking at me when you think I won't notice."

"Do they hurt?"

She glanced over at him, saw the remorse on his face. She didn't have to ask what "they" he was talking about. "A little. It's manageable, though."

"I'm sorry they used you to get to me."

"That helps a little." She returned his smile.

They were silent for another half hour as Daeva got them back onto the main road. So far, they hadn't been followed by the Cabal.

A yawn escaped her lips as she put the car on cruise control. She was tired, which was a new sensation. Normally she could go for days without having to rest, but obviously being out and being human-ish made her body desire rest and recuperation time.

Yawning again, she tried to hide it behind a hand, but Quinn noticed.

"You need to rest."

She shook her head. "No, I'm sure it's just a strange reaction to being topside."

"Daeva, you need to sleep. It'll help you heal."

"Yeah, but aren't you tired?"

"I can go another five hours." He pointed to a rest stop. "Pull over there, and we can switch."

She did, and she moved into the passenger seat as Quinn took up as the driver. When they were back on the road, she rested her head against the glass of the window. Her eyes were heavy, and eventually they drooped. Then, for the first time in years, she drifted off to sleep and dreamed.

The sunlight streamed in through the kitchen window and played across Quinn's face as he grated parmesan cheese. He was smiling and there was a little dimple in his right cheek.

She couldn't resist. Daeva reached up and smoothed her finger over it. "So damn cute."

That had him smiling harder, and he took her hand in his and pressed his lips to her fingertips. "I can't finish this if you keep touching me."

She got up from the stool she'd been sitting on at the kitchen island and came up behind him, wrapping her arms around his chest. She splayed her fingers over the hard muscular plane.

"Then don't finish."

He chuckled. "I thought you were hungry."

"Just for you." She nibbled on his shoulder, her favorite spot.

He dropped the grater, spun and grabbed her around the buttocks. He lifted her and set her down right next to the cheese he'd been grating.

"Spaghetti Bolognese is so overrated anyway," he said as he nibbled on her chin.

"I totally agree."

She wrapped her hands in his hair as he took her mouth. It didn't matter how many times he'd kissed her before, it still sent jolts of pleasure zinging through her. He was skilled with his tongue and teeth and lips, making her head spin.

He ran his hands through her hair, then down her back, pressing her close. He nuzzled into her ear and spoke the words she'd been longing to hear.

"I love you."

She pulled his head back and looked into his face. *"I love you, too,"* she answered back with the same words, words she'd never spoken to another in her entire life. She kissed him hard, her love for him overwhelming her completely.

With clever fingers, he had her skirt pushed up and her panties off before she took another *breath. Laughing, she wrapped her legs around his waist.*

"You're a naughty boy, Quinn Strom," she panted as she nuzzled into him.

"You don't know the half of it."

Then he was buried deep inside her.

Daeva jolted awake, hitting her head on the passenger side window. She sat up and wiped at her chin. Drool had dribbled there.

She stretched out her neck, then glanced over at Quinn. He was looking at her funny.

"What?"

"Were you dreaming?"

She frowned. "Why?"

"No reason." He put his attention back on the road.

Had she talked in her sleep? The dream had felt so real, she wouldn't have been surprised if she had said something out loud. Anyway, it wasn't so much a dream as it was a memory. That had been when Quinn had asked her to move in with him—after they'd had sex in the kitchen, eaten dinner, then made love later in bed with wine and candlelight.

It had been one of the happiest moments of her life.

When she'd come topside to live a life, she'd never, ever expected to fall in love. All she'd wanted to do was live a normal life as a human. She'd been lucky to have found Rachel near death in a coma. Daeva had been able to give her body another chance to live. Rachel's mind had been damaged, enough that she never regained consciousness, so Daeva didn't have to quiet her when she moved in. Falling for Quinn had been an unexpected but pleasant surprise.

Daeva stretched her legs and looked out at the dark road. "Where are we?"

"Somewhere in Oregon. I got off the interstate just in case we're still being followed."

She watched his profile, searching for the dimple she knew was there. He yawned and rubbed at his eyes.

"Why don't I drive for a while? You look tired."

"How's your shoulder?"

She tested it by rotating her arm. There was still a deep ache but it was nothing compared to the pain before. "It's good."

"Good." He yawned again. "There's a rest stop just ahead. We can switch there."

At the turnoff, he pulled over. They switched

duties, Quinn opting for the back seat to stretch out in.

Daeva pulled out onto the road and set the cruise control. She turned on the radio, quickly finding a station. The first beats of "Viva Las Vegas" came out of the speakers.

She chuckled.

"What?" Quinn asked from the backseat.

"I was just thinking about that time we did a road trip to Vegas and you kept playing this song over and over again."

He was silent for a moment and she thought maybe he didn't hear her, or maybe he didn't want to answer, but then he said, "I remember."

"I got so sick of that song that…"

"You threw the CD out the window while we were on the interstate."

"Yeah." She laughed. "I thought you were going to get mad but instead you slid in another annoying CD."

"Johnny Cash."

She shook her head, still laughing. "I never could understand your love of fifties music."

He was silent after that. She glanced in the rearview mirror and saw that his eyes were closed. She watched him off and on for a few minutes as his chest rose and fell steadily. He was asleep.

Smiling to herself, she turned up the volume a little and started to sing along to the song.

Chapter 10

As he slept, Quinn dreamed about the first time he'd seen Daeva. She'd been Rachel at the time but that didn't make her any less potent. He'd been on a job and she'd been the right girl at the wrong time.

Friday night the Shark Club was bursting at the seams with people. Quinn sat at the bar nursing a soda water and lime as he surveyed the crowd for his quarry. Not a demon this time, but a sorcerer named Todd who liked to call demons to do his dirty work. The sorcerer was part of the Crimson Hall Cabal and a badass.

Or so he thought. Quinn had dealt with the guy before, so he knew who to watch for and what to watch for. The sorcerer liked to pick up drunk women; blondes were his favorite flavor. And there was a smorgasbord available in this club.

Quinn didn't have to wait too long before he spied the sorcerer cozying up to a table of ladies, two of them blonde, the others a brunette and a redhead. The sorcerer pulled up a chair and sat down. Luckily his back was to the room, so Quinn would have the advantage of stealth. He could sneak up on his quarry and take the sorcerer by surprise, hopefully avoiding anyone getting in the way or getting hurt.

Leaving his soda at the bar, Quinn pushed through the crowd toward the table. When he reached it, Todd was leaning toward one blonde, whispering something into her ear. She didn't look all that impressed.

Quinn put his hand on Todd's shoulder and bent down to speak quietly. "Let's go outside for a little talk."

Todd flinched and quickly glanced back at Quinn. In an instant, recognition filled his eyes. And he reacted.

Pushing to his feet, he swung an arm and

backhanded Quinn across the face. It was a hard hit, intensified by the telltale glow of magic. A jolt sang down Quinn's body, making his knees ineffectual. He dropped to the floor, the back of his head making a resonating smack on the hardwood.

Black dots clouded his vision. He blinked them back. When he could finally see clearly, a slim hand came into view. He looked past it to the owner and lost his breath all over again.

She smiled down at him. "Need a hand up?"

She was radiant, with long blond hair that flowed around her pale face like sunshine. Her eyes were a piercing blue that speared him to the core. Her smile was genuine and full of good humor.

He let her pull him up. When they were face-to-face, her tantalizing scent filled his nose. Every part of his body responded to it. He had yet to relinquish his hold on her hand.

"You might have a bruise in the morning." She lightly brushed his cheek with her fingertips. An electrifying jolt sizzled down his spine.

All thoughts of Todd drained from his mind. This woman had taken up the space.

"Can I buy you a drink?" he asked her.

"No, but you can buy me breakfast in the morning. I'm already starving." She tugged on his hand and together they left the club.

That had been the beginning of a three-year love affair that Quinn still ached for.

"Quinn?" A hand touched his leg and he jolted awake.

Blinking back sleep, he looked at that slim hand then up at those devastating eyes. So much the same. But different.

"What?" Sitting up, he rubbed at his face, trying to brush off the remnants of his vivid dream. So vivid that her scent was still caught in his nostrils. "Are we close to the border?"

"No, not really."

He looked out the window and saw the pancake house that was connected to a motel. "Why are we stopped here?"

"Because I need me some pancakes with strawberries and whipped cream. And I thought we could both use the rest. We could get a room with one of those Magic Fingers beds."

She turned off the car.

He sighed, exasperation filling him. "We don't have time for this, Daeva."

"We're off the grid. The Cabal doesn't know where we are." She opened the door. "And I'm pretty sure you'd just about kill for some stuffed French toast." She got out of the car, slamming the door shut on any argument he could give.

His stomach grumbled. He could eat. And stuffed French toast was, indeed, his favorite. It figured that she would remember that and then throw it in his face.

He opened the door and followed her into the restaurant.

Once they were seated and had ordered, Quinn relaxed a little. The smell of coffee, butter and grease always filled him with a sense of the familiar. He and his dad, and sometimes Ivy, often used a place like this as a meeting place during a hunt. Or as the place they went to celebrate after a successful one.

He'd taken Daeva, when she'd been Rachel, to one of these for their first breakfast date. She'd had pancakes with strawberries and whipped cream.

Quinn played with the salt and pepper shakers as they waited for their food.

"So, how's Ronan?"

His fingers stilled. "You know Ronan?"

"Yeah, he used to call me all the time."

"Did he?"

"Yup." She leaned on the table. "You're not jealous, are you?"

"Of course not," he sputtered. "Besides, Ronan is with Ivy now."

Her eyes widened. "Really? Well, I guess I should have seen that coming. They seemed pretty cozy last time I saw them."

"When did you see them?"

"During all that trouble in Sumner that went on."

"You knew about that?"

"Honey, everyone knew about that little war. It was the talk of the town for weeks down under." She picked at her napkin. "Ronan summoned me to help him find a demon that needed killing."

"That was nice of you."

"Yeah, I thought so."

Quinn had tried to put Sumner behind him. He still blamed himself for what happened. If he hadn't been hiding out in that small town, demons wouldn't have come looking for him, and they wouldn't have possessed a lot of the townfolk and pitted neighbor against neighbor in a bloody war for his head. He'd seen a lot of people die in that town. Strangers and friends.

The waitress arrived with their food. Before she even left the table, Daeva was chowing down.

"I'm so hungry. Who knew being bound to the Earth made a demon so darn hungry all the time?"

A spot of strawberry juice dotted the side of her full mouth as she chewed. He had to fight the urge to reach across the table and wipe it away with the pad of his thumb. Instead, he put his attention onto consuming his delicious French toast without seeming like a glutton.

He tried to avoid looking at her while she ate. Her face was all lit up with delight as she devoured her pancakes. She licked her fork after each bite, gathering every bit of syrup and strawberry sauce she could get. It reminded him a bit of a child discovering candy or chocolate for the first time. A look of pure joy.

When his lips threatened to twitch upward into a smile, he grabbed his coffee and drank.

She set her fork down and, leaning back in the booth, sighed contentedly. "That was better than I remembered."

"Can't get pancakes in hell?"

"Nope. The goblins have no concept of light and fluffy. Or sweet, for that matter." She wiped her face with the napkin. "Now I need a nap."

"We should really press on."

She shook her head. "I can't. I need to heal, Quinn." She moved her shoulder and he could see the pain on her face. "I'm no good to you if I'm not one hundred percent. If we get attacked again, I can't guarantee I can save your life."

He sighed and pushed his plate away.

"Besides, you could use the sleep, as well. It doesn't look like you've slept in days."

After paying the bill, they made their way over to the motel office to rent a room. The moment Quinn unlocked the door to their ground-floor abode, Daeva stumbled in, shuffled to the bed and collapsed on top of it. She reached behind her, grabbed the blanket and flipped it over her body. Tucking one hand under her chin, she closed her eyes.

"Got any change for the Magic Fingers?" she mumbled sleepily.

After setting the bags on the table, he dug into his pants pocket and came away with a few coins. He flipped them to her.

She snatched them out of the air without even opening her eyes.

"Cool trick."

She smiled, then opened her eyes to slide the money into the metal box on the side table. "I have my moments."

The massager kicked in and jiggled the bed violently. Daeva groaned. "Now, that's what I'm talking about."

Quinn pulled a chair up to the table, sat and rummaged through his bag for his knives and whetstone. He thought he might as well make use of the wasted time to prepare for the next leg of their journey. He needed to keep his wits and hone his weapons. Who knew what they would come up against? More sorcerers, certainly, but he wouldn't be surprised if they also came up against demons.

Unfortunately he didn't know anyone he could call to help them. A lot of hunters he knew were dead, some killed in the war in Sumner, and others were entangled with their own demons, literally and figuratively. Alcoholism was an epidemic in his line of work.

He glanced at Daeva and wondered if she would fight against her own. Did she harbor any loyalty for her own kind? Did she have family? Friends?

"What's it like in hell?" he asked, before he could think better of it.

She opened her eyes and stared at him. "Are you asking to bother me so I can't sleep, or do you really want to know?"

"I want to know."

Tucking the blanket tighter over her shoulder, she closed her eyes again. At first, Quinn thought she wasn't going to answer him, but then she started to talk.

"The stories of fire and brimstone are true. Everything stinks to high heaven of sulfur. It's always hot in the honeycomb."

"The honeycomb?"

"Yeah, it's shaped like that. Many levels that open up to the center, which is the fiery pit. The place where souls are tortured for an eternity. Doesn't matter where you go, that's always there. It's a daily reminder that hell exists. You can smell the burned flesh and hear the strangled cries of tortured souls 24/7." She shuddered under the blanket.

"I can't imagine."

"No. You can't."

"Do you have your own…ah, place?"

"Yes, it's like a small apartment. I have a few luxuries, like books, and my goblin friends Loir and her brother Klix. They take care of me. I'm luckier than most because of my level two status. Most demons, those in the lower levels, live in squalor, in dormitories, I guess you'd call them. All scrambling for scraps of food and comfort.

"It's what I see and hear every day that torments me, though. The stench of burning flesh and the screams of the damned can really get to a girl, you know? Thankfully I'm not forced to participate anymore. I did my time in the pits."

He stared at her, unsure of what to say. He had no idea what it was truly like in hell. There had always been stories, he'd even heard some accounts from other hunters, but obviously those had been lies. He wasn't sure exactly what he thought demons did in hell, but he certainly never thought of it like a prison for them. The souls that were condemned there certainly, but not its residents.

She opened her eyes and he witnessed the horror in them. "Now you know why I would do anything not to be in that…hell." She rolled over on the bed, wrapping herself tightly in the blanket like a cocoon. "If you'll excuse me, I need to sleep."

He watched her for a few minutes more before setting his blade and whetstone on the table, then standing. He had to get some air. The room had gotten progressively stifling and uncomfortable as she talked. He was having trouble breathing.

Sliding a knife into his belt sheath, he grabbed the key and left, shutting the door quietly behind him. Just outside, he took in some deep breaths of the fresh, untainted air.

He walked around the motel trying to shake the images Daeva's words had planted in his mind. In his lifetime, he'd seen a lot of death and destruction and horror but nothing compared to what shc'd experienced every day of her life. For more years than he could even comprehend. To be forced to live with that, in that, and have no escape.

He stopped walking and took in another deep breath. Would he do whatever he could to escape that situation? Lie? Cheat? Steal? Possess? Hell, yeah. He had no doubt.

And the only escape afforded a demon was

possession. He understood that now. He understood why Daeva had chosen to possess Rachel for so long. Like a woman in hiding from an abusive husband, she had escaped and hidden from her tormentor. Which was her origin. Hell.

By the time he made it back around to the motel room, he was tired. The last few days were catching up with him. Daeva had been right that he needed rest, as well. But he couldn't go back into the room. There was this needling sensation in his gut. And he was pretty sure it was guilt. A feeling he didn't really want to deal with right now.

So, instead of facing it, he opened the car's back door and crawled in. He settled his head on the armrest and shut his eyes. He'd deal with it all later, but right now he just wanted some peace.

Chapter 11

A knock on the car window jolted him awake. Stretching, Quinn sat up and looked at Daeva, who was smiling at him through the backseat window. He bounced across the seat and, opening the door, slid out of the car.

She handed him a coffee she'd obviously gotten from the restaurant. "Morning, sunshine."

He just grunted at her and took a needful sip of hot coffee. It chased away some of the haunting images he still had in his head.

"You don't look so good. Did you get any sleep?"

"Some."

"Why didn't you sleep in the room?"

He gave her a look. "You hogged the whole bed."

"Oh." She shrugged. "Sorry about that."

"Yeah, I'm pretty sure you're not too sorry."

She gave him a saucy grin. "You'd be right." She went around to the trunk, popped it and tossed their bags inside. "I already checked us out. So we're ready to go." She opened the passenger door and slid in.

After three hours on the road they'd edged closer to the border crossing. Quinn looked at Daeva casually flipping through a fashion magazine she'd gotten earlier at the motel shop.

"You never did explain to me how you plan to get across the border without a passport or any type of ID."

"Drop me off before the border crossing. I'll get across."

He was silent for a moment, considering that. Was she trying to ditch him? Trying to wiggle her way out of their deal?

As if reading his thoughts, she said, "I can't leave you, remember? I'm bound to you."

"How are you going to get across?"

"I think I can still be invisible. No one will see me. I'll meet you on the other side. Just pull off the road about half a mile from the crossing."

Quinn wasn't so sure about the plan but he couldn't think of an alternative. He had to trust that she would do as she said. He did bind her to him during the ritual, but that didn't mean she couldn't take her sweet time in showing back up.

"Okay. I need to eat and use the bathroom, anyway."

"We should probably fill up, too."

After another ten minutes, Quinn pulled the car off the road and into a gas station. As he went inside, she pumped the gas.

He used the facilities, thankful for a reprieve from Daeva. He had a lot of conflicting emotions racing around inside. It proved difficult to consolidate the woman he'd loved for years with the demon-ness he'd vowed to hate. That hate was quickly fading away.

So used to everything being black and white, Quinn only saw human good, demon bad. There was no middle ground. But that had started to change when his sister, Ivy, had fallen in love with a cambion. Ronan was half-human, half-demon and completely in love with Ivy. He'd sacrificed everything he'd ever wanted in life for her.

Quinn had even grown to like the guy, for that sacrifice alone. He'd never admit it to Ronan or Ivy, but he wouldn't put up a fight at all if they decided to get married.

He was starting to realize that just because someone was a demon didn't automatically make them evil or bad or wrong. And that thinking messed up everything he'd worked out about Daeva over the past few years. Seeing her, being with her, respecting her, messed it up even more.

As he stood in line to pay for the gas and two sub sandwiches, he watched Daeva as she finished filling the tank and set the nozzle back in the cradle. The light played across her hair, making it shine like newly minted copper pennies. She lifted her face to the sun and a smile spread her lips. Not for the first time, Quinn thought about capturing those lips with his own. He wondered if she would taste the same, feel the same in his arms.

She turned her head and their gazes met through the window. Her smile widened. His gut churned and he returned his focus to the cashier ringing up his purchases.

He had to force himself to remember that this was not a road trip to Vegas. Daeva was not the woman he fell in love with six years ago. This was strictly a business arrangement. He needed the chest and she knew where it was. It was that simple. He had to stop his emotions from complicating the situation.

Just because he sympathized with her desire to be out of hell didn't absolve her from past mistakes. He supposed it wasn't her actual possession that had angered him, it was that she never trusted him enough to tell him.

Resolved to keep his emotions about the past and present in check, he grabbed the subs and headed back to the car.

They ate and drove in silence the rest of the way. About a half mile from the border crossing, Quinn pulled over to the side of the road.

"I'm not keen on this plan," he said.

"Neither am I. I'm not a big fan of hiking through the wilderness. But it's not like I have Jedi mind tricks. I lost my mind mojo when you bound me to this plane and to you."

"But you still have your invisibility cloak?"

Friday nights had been their movie night. Daeva had a penchant for sci-fi films and Harry Potter.

She smiled. "Sort of. Enough that I can get by unnoticed. If someone was specifically looking for me, a demon named Daeva, well, then I'd stick out like a sore thumb."

"Okay. Once I'm through, I'll pull over to the side of the road. I'll pretend I'm having a picnic in the great Canadian outdoors."

She went to open the door, then looked at him. "You know, I'm more worried about how you're getting across. Last time I remember, Quinn Strom had a warrant or two out for his arrest."

He held up a passport. "That's why I'm Todd Sheppard today."

She laughed. "You stole that sorcerer's identity?"

"Yup. Years ago. Believe it or not he's squeaky clean and even pays his taxes ahead of time."

She shook her head, but he could tell she was extremely amused by the turn of events.

"Stay safe," she said.

"You, too."

She slid out and shut the door. Before any of the people in the other vehicles coming up the highway could spot her, she dashed into the thicket of trees. He saw one flash of red through the greenery, and then she was gone.

The line of vehicles at the border stop wasn't long. Twenty minutes and Quinn was pulling up to the guard post. He rolled down his window and handed his passport to the uniformed woman inside.

She took it, scanned the number, looked at the computer screen, then at him. "Where are you headed, Mr. Sheppard?"

"Kelowna."

"What is the purpose of your visit?"

"Pleasure. Taking a little vacation. Going to do some camping."

She glanced into the back of the vehicle, likely spying the backpack and gear. She looked back at him for a long moment before turning back to the screen. She typed for a minute, then with his passport in hand, she stood.

"Please pull up into one of those stalls, sir."

"Is there some problem?"

"Just do it, sir."

Heart thudding, Quinn drove the car forward

and parked in front of a long glass-and-brick building. Something was definitely wrong. He could've been pulled out randomly from the long line of cars, certainly, but he didn't think so. There was something in the way the officer had looked at him. And he'd swear he saw a slight smirk on her lips and a flash of inky black in her eyes.

Chapter 12

Daeva was wearing the wrong footwear for hiking through the woods. Already her feet hurt and she'd only been walking for forty minutes. Through the trees, she could see the immigration building and the lineup of vehicles leading to it.

She looked for Quinn but couldn't see the car. He'd probably already gone through. She just hoped his passport held up. Using another person's identity was risky, to say the least. Maybe that person had just gotten arrested for assault or murder. Using their ID then would be a huge mistake.

But it wouldn't have surprised Daeva if Quinn had kept records on the sorcerer. The exorcist was usually thorough when it came to his job, which really was his life.

Because of that, it had always surprised her that Quinn had never realized she'd been possessing Rachel's body. It had taken her moment of truth to reveal her secret to him. Maybe love had blinded him to the truth.

She supposed, in retrospect, she shouldn't have been surprised when he reacted the way he did. She'd been foolish to think that he'd loved her enough to overlook the fact that she was a demon living in a human vessel. Obviously, love had made *her* delusional.

Daeva kicked a rock out of her way as she tramped through the trees. She stepped onto a rotted log and got stuck, her boot heel wedged inside. Frustrated, she wrenched her leg, trying to pull her foot out. It didn't come at first, then let go with an audible snap. She looked down and saw she'd broken the heel right off her boot.

"Perfect," she grunted.

She continued the trek through the trees,

limping on the broken heel, which made it that much more difficult to walk through the brush. As she passed, the tip of a gnarled branch snagged a strand of her hair and pulled it from her ponytail. She stopped to put it back in place.

As she pulled the elastic from her hair, a sense of dread washed over her. Swinging around, she stared into the woods. Was an animal stalking her? She felt as though something was deathly wrong. Her gut clenched into a tight ball.

Her gaze moved over the trees, stopping briefly on a chipmunk chattering and a robin feeding her young in the nest she'd built high in the trees. Then she looked at the building separating the two countries. A cold fist wrapped around her heart and squeezed until she couldn't breathe. Something was wrong. Quinn was in trouble. Like the cold, she could sense it all the way to her bones.

She smoothed her hair back into a tight ponytail and stepped out of the trees. After mumbling a quick incantation, Daeva moved out onto the road. The quick spell made her unseen. Not quite invisible. She could be seen if someone was looking for her. But to those who weren't, she was like a shadow that moves in the corner of a person's eye. There, but not quite.

Before she made her way across the tarmac, she took off her boots. It would be easier to go barefoot. She moved around the vehicles slowly creeping forward to the crossing gate. A young child in a baby seat reached for her through the open window as she passed. Children could see more than most adults.

"Hi." The little boy waved as she went past his window.

Daeva turned to him and put her finger to her lips. "Shhh."

His smile faded and he tucked his arm back into the car.

As she neared the gate, she spotted their car in the lot. So Quinn had obviously been stopped. But why? She knew he would've been extremely careful when talking to the immigration officer. So that meant either Mr. Todd Sheppard had done something wrong and his passport had been flagged, or worse, someone knew where they were headed and why.

When she reached the car, she opened the back door and grabbed both of Quinn's bags. They instantly became as invisible as she was.

She was surprised they hadn't been confiscated. If this had been a normal inspection, the officers would've taken them inside to be searched. Obviously, this wasn't a normal inspection.

Bags in hand, she went around to the side of the building. She unzipped one. There had to be something inside that could help her. There were clothes, two knives, some holy water ampoules and what looked like two smoke bombs. Perfect.

She snagged the holy water and the canisters, settling them into her jacket pockets. She had a feeling they would come in handy. Setting her shoulders, she took a deep breath, opened the door to the customs building, determined to find Quinn and bust him out.

Chapter 13

There were only two pieces of furniture in the small, dreary room: the folding metal chair Quinn sat in and the cold metal table in front of him. The chair was uncomfortable, but he figured that was its purpose.

Without any explanation, he'd been led to the room, told to sit and wait. He'd asked a million questions, like why was he being detained, and what was this was all about. But the officer remained stoic and tight-lipped.

Basically he knew he was up shit creek without a paddle. He didn't even have his bags. The only thing on him was a small silver knife strapped to his ankle and a small ampoule of holy water in his front pants pocket. He sensed he'd need both of those things soon enough. Because he was pretty certain the officer in charge was possessed.

The door opened and said officer walked in. She still had that little smirk on her ruddy, pinched face. It was the kind of look that said she knew everything and that he'd better be afraid.

She stood on the other side of the table and leaned forward, leering at him. "So, Mr. Strom, where exactly are you going?"

"I'm sorry. I think you have me confused with someone else. My name's Todd Sheppard."

Smiling, the officer shook her head. "I don't think so." She leaned even farther. "You see, I know the sniveling little sorcerer. And you ain't him." Inky black bled into her brown eyes and her wide grin grew maniacal and grotesque.

Yup, she was definitely possessed.

He had to play it cool if he wanted to get out of here unscathed. As if interested in what she had to say, Quinn also leaned forward. The movement gave him a better chance to get the holy water ampoule out of his pocket unnoticed.

"I told you, I'm just going camping."

She sniffed. "You don't really seem like the outdoorsy type."

"Oh, I am. I love it. Clean air, surrounded by nature. It's awesome."

"We know you recently summoned Daeva, the Seductress of Shadows, and temporarily released her from hell. For what purpose?"

Quinn smiled. "We're in a relationship. Didn't you know? Have been for years. I missed her, is all."

This had the guard straightening. She almost looked nervous. "Then where is Daeva?"

His fingers gripped the ampoule in his pocket. He slowly drew it out, careful not to give his intentions away. "Oh, she's probably around here somewhere." He hoped.

He didn't want to entertain the thought that Daeva may have tried to bail on him. But it was there at the back of his mind, regardless. She'd have reason to. He hadn't been the kindest person toward her. He wouldn't blame her if she wanted to leave him here to the torturous hands of these demons. She couldn't, of course, because of the binding. She would be compelled to stay close by. Whether she did anything to get him out would be another thing altogether.

"If you don't tell me why you are crossing into Canada, I'm going to hurt you."

He grinned. "Do your worst."

But when the officer produced a taser from her belt, his smile faded. That was the last thing he'd expected. A few well-placed punches to the face and body he could handle; even a few deep cuts were tolerable. But electricity running through his body was a whole different matter. He'd been tasered before and it was awful.

"Last chance, Strom, to be reasonable."

He palmed the holy water then spread his arms out wide to the sides. "Hey, I've never been a reasonable guy. You should know that by now."

She picked up the taser and aimed but Quinn was faster.

He threw the glass vial hard at the officer's face. It broke on impact, splashing holy water into her eyes and across her cheek. Tendrils of black smoke instantly rose from her burning flesh.

Shrieking, she raised her hands to her eyes.

This afforded Quinn time to bolt from the chair and get to the door. But when he cranked on the handle it was locked.

"Shit!"

He looked back at the possessed officer as she continued to screech and wipe at her burning eyes. She had to have a key.

Heart thudding, he raced back to her and pulled at her belt, trying to get it off. She slapped and clawed at him as he unbuckled the strap.

Nails raked across his cheek and forearm, leaving deep divots. He worked past the pain and continued to struggle with the clasp until he had it undone and was pulling the belt out from the loops. The keys hung from a ring latched to one metal ring.

"You're dead, Quinn Strom," she shrieked, her voice guttural and deep. The demon inside was pissed off and trying to get out of its host.

Instead of staying to debate that statement, Quinn found the right key and unlocked the door. He bolted out into the corridor just as a smoking metal canister came sailing through the air toward his head.

"Duck!"

Quinn dropped to his knees. The canister

skimmed the top of his head. It landed just outside the interrogation room door, billowing thick white smoke into the air. Hand over his nose and mouth, he jumped back to his feet and ran down the corridor toward Daeva, who waited for him, the second smoke bomb in her hand ready to go.

When he reached her side, she tossed him one of his bags. "Let's get the hell out of here. There are two more possessed coming down the hall."

He wrapped the bag strap around his shoulders, then he noticed she was barefoot. "Ah, what happened to your boots?"

"Long story. Tell you later." She turned to move down the hall toward the main doors. Shaking his head, he followed her out.

Their escape went mostly unhindered. They didn't run into anyone until they reached the front doors. A young female officer was the only thing between them and freedom.

"Stop right here." She held up her taser, her hand noticeably shaking.

"Look," Daeva said, "just let us go. If you don't, you're going to get hurt. I really don't want to hurt you. I'm trying to turn over a new leaf."

Quinn put his hand out toward the girl, who

really couldn't be any older than twenty. "This isn't your fight. Just turn away and let us go."

She looked from Daeva to Quinn then back again. "This is my first day of work." Her voice shook.

Quinn could tell she was scared out of her mind. "Don't make it your last. We're not worth it. Trust me. We're not terrorists."

Tears brimming in her eyes, she lowered the taser.

"Thank you," Daeva said, as she brushed past the guard to reach the door.

Quinn followed, but paused with his hand on the door. He glanced back at the young officer. "What size are your shoes?"

"What?" she stammered.

"Your shoes. What size?"

"Ah, seven."

"Give them to me, please."

Daeva came to his side. "What are you doing? We need to get the hell out of here."

"Getting you some shoes."

She gave him a small smile as the officer toed off her shoes. "Wow, Quinn, who knew you were such a romantic."

He grabbed up the shoes and handed them to her. "Don't ever say I never got you anything."

Daeva laughed, then, clutching the shoes to her chest, burst out the door with Quinn right on her bare heels.

Chapter 14

As soon as they were clear of the building, Daeva stopped to put the shoes on. She hated it that her heart thumped just a little bit harder because Quinn had stopped to get her a pair. He probably had no idea how endearing that was. He'd likely been thinking about practicality, about how it would slow them up if she had to tiptoe her way through the woods.

Despite all that, she still found it cute, and it reminded her of the old Quinn. The one she'd been in love with. The tender, compassionate man who used to bring her flowers just because he was thinking of her.

Once she had the shoes on, they sprinted into the trees separating the two countries. They'd have to make a run for it. Stay in the trees as long as possible and then reach the town of Osoyoos, where they could steal transportation and get the hell out of there.

Quinn had his compass out. "The town is northeast of here. We should be able to make it in an hour." He chucked the compass back into his pack. "All right. Let's move."

He ran at a quick, directed pace. Daeva was able to keep stride. Fortunately the shoes were sturdy and comfortable, even without socks, and didn't give her blisters the way her boots had. It was funny to think of a demon with blisters on her feet. She did live in a fiery pit of despair. The word out there was that demons were indestructible. But that was so untrue. Especially for one bound to the Earth and to an exorcist. Daeva could suffer just as much as everyone else. In some ways, even more. She tired more quickly and had been healing more slowly. But she couldn't tell Quinn.

After about twenty minutes of solid running,

Quinn stopped to drink from his canteen. He offered it to her and she took it, drinking gratefully. He had to pry it from her hand to stop her from emptying it.

"Don't drink too much or you'll get sick."

"Damn, I hate this thirst and hunger all the time. I'd totally forgotten how much sustenance a human body needs to survive."

"Yeah, it sucks sometimes." He took another swig, then capped the canteen.

"So, what happened in there?"

"The officer at the gate was possessed. It was as if she'd been waiting for me."

"Could have been. Although I'd imagine there are possessed guards at every border stop."

"They knew I'd summoned and released you."

"Of course. We are tagged, to an extent. No one leaves hell without someone noticing."

"But they don't know where we're going or why."

"Well, that's something at least."

He looked at her, searching her face. "You never told anyone about the chest?"

"No. Not in one hundred years."

"Why did you tell me?"

She met his gaze straight on, hoping he saw the feelings she still had for him. She couldn't deny that they continued to exist. "Because I trusted you." She shrugged, lightening the mood. "It was a momentary lack of judgment. I'm sure it won't happen again."

He smiled. "Oh, it probably will."

"Yeah." She nodded, her lips twitching up. "Probably."

He stared at her in the eyes for a long moment. "Thanks for coming for me."

"It looked like you were doing fine all on your own."

He lifted his chin. "Yeah, I was, but it was nice to have backup just in case."

She returned his smile. "You're welcome."

Decidedly uncomfortable, Quinn shifted his weight from foot to foot as she surveyed the trees behind him. "I don't hear dogs or anything. Maybe we're in the clear."

"I wouldn't count on that. They'll use demon magic to track us. Use the animals around us to keep eyes on the prize."

He rubbed a hand over the stubble on his chin.

"So what's the plan when we reach town?" she asked.

"Steal a vehicle and get back on the road."

"I think we should stay off the main highway and out of hotels. Either we sleep in the car or in a tent."

He nodded. "I agree." He checked the compass direction again. "Okay, let's keep moving. Town should just be over that rise."

Quinn had almost been right about the location of the community. It was over the rise, then down into a valley near a lake. It took them close to another hour before they reached the town limits.

Osoyoos was a small town and definitely a tourist destination, which totally worked for them as neither looked like they were locals. They made their way downtown to scout out vehicles.

As they strolled the main street searching for the greatest concentration of cars, Daeva was conscious of Quinn looking at her. Shifting the duffel bag to her other shoulder, she turned to him.

"What? You keep looking at me."

"You kind of stand out."

"What? Why?" She stopped to look at her reflection in a store window. "Is there something on my face?" Despite a dirt smudge on her cheek she couldn't see anything out of the ordinary. She rubbed at it as she turned to face Quinn again.

"Everyone's staring at you."

She frowned but did start to notice that almost every guy who walked by did a double take. A few women did, as well.

"Well, I'm sorry. This is my face. This is what I look like. I can't help it."

He chuckled. "You almost sound sad for being so pretty."

She stopped rubbing at her cheek. "You think I'm pretty?"

Quinn dropped his gaze and started walking again. She had to rush to keep up. "Let's just find a car and get out of here."

"Hey, you're the one that made a point of it."

"Yeah, because we can hardly blend in when you look like…"

She put her hand on her hip. "Look like what?"

He stopped and glared at her, as if it was all her fault. "Like sex on a stick, okay?"

"Oh." She was a bit taken aback by his anger.

He sounded so miserable that he found her attractive. It was almost comical.

She pulled the elastic from her hair. "Well, does this help?" She put her hands in her hair and mussed it all up.

He watched her with interest, then frowned more deeply, his eyes going dark. "No. That's worse."

Desperate, she looked around and spied a tourist shop with a few racks standing just outside their open door. She went to it, grabbed a baseball cap with a Canadian flag on it and put it on.

"There. Does that make a difference?"

"No, now you just look like a hot girl in a bad hat." He shook his head and grabbed the hat off her head to put it back. "Let's just get off the main drag and find a parking lot where we can jack a vehicle."

"Fine," she huffed, following him down the sidewalk.

Leave it to Quinn to make her looks a detriment to their mission. As if she had any control over them. Didn't he realize that his sexy darkness made it difficult for her to concentrate as well? He should be apologizing to her for having the perfect ass and beautiful shoulders that she always wanted to sink her teeth into. And lips that made her melt with every thought of them being on her skin, kissing her, nibbling on her. It was totally unfair that he made her quiver with possibilities. How could she focus on the mission when all she wanted to do was sink into him, to lose herself completely in everything about him?

When he noticed she wasn't right beside him, Quinn stopped walking and turned around. "Are you coming or what?"

"Yeah, I'm coming. Quit being so damned bossy."

They found a parking lot behind the strip of mom-and-pop businesses. There were about fifteen vehicles parked in the small, cramped space. Some of them were for customers and others for employees. Their best bet was an employee vehicle that wouldn't be discovered missing as quickly. Hopefully not until the end of the day. By then, they would be long gone.

Daeva didn't think the choices looked all that promising: two trucks, both having seen better days, one Smart Car, one Toyota with anti-theft on it and a motorcycle. If their circumstances were different, she would've voted for the bike, but they still needed to get some camping gear and there was no way it would fit on the back with the two of them. Same went for the Smart Car, however adorable it was. That basically left the two pickups.

"I vote for the blue one. It doesn't look as grungy as the other one."

"Stealers can't be choosers," Quinn said with a grin.

She knew he totally loved this part of the job. She suspected if he hadn't been an exorcist and demon hunter, doing the good work, he would have ended up some sort of criminal, likely a car thief. She remembered how he was when he was out doing a job. He'd always return home amped up and wanting to bury himself in her for hours.

After being together for a few months, he'd told her about what he did. She of course had already known. All demons, topside and downside, knew who Quinn Strom was. But she'd put on a good act about being surprised. She'd just been so happy that he'd trusted her enough to tell her. It was around then when she'd fallen in love with him.

"Keep a lookout," he told her as he slid a metal jimmy out of his duffel bag.

She watched the area for any sign of trouble as Quinn slid the metal bar between the window and the doorjamb. After a few seconds, she heard the telltale clicking sound of a lock being disengaged. She turned around to see Quinn sliding into the cab on his back so he could break the ignition panel and hotwire the vehicle. It didn't take him long to get it started. He was certainly skilled in the criminal arts.

Sitting up he glanced at her and mouthed, *Let's go*.

With one last cursory glance down the alley, Daeva went around to the passenger side, opened the door and jumped in.

"I saw a sporting goods store at the edge of town when we first came in. We can get the gear we need there."

"Do you have enough money?" she asked.

"There should be about three grand in that bag. I also have four credit cards, in case of emergencies."

She smiled, he was like a Boy Scout—always prepared.

They reached the store without incident.

Once inside, Quinn looked to her. "This is your excursion, what do we need?"

"A tent, sleeping bags, flashlight, food, water, proper hiking boots, warm jackets, gloves and probably a pickax."

He lifted an eyebrow. "A pickax?"

She nodded. "Trust me, we'll need it."

"So, how far north are we going?"

"Far enough that, although it's summer, we're going to need those jackets."

Without another word, Quinn grabbed a cart and started tossing things in.

By the time they were done, they had a truck-load of gear, including a couple of backpacks to carry it all in. Quinn's duffel bags wouldn't do for where they needed to go.

When they were back in the truck and on the road, Quinn tossed her a map of British Columbia. "Okay, navigator, where to?"

She unfolded it on her lap and stared at all the lines and dots. She didn't need a map to know where they were going, but she knew it would help Quinn in a way, to ease his mind and give him back some control. She traced a finger over the paper, up and up, and stopped it on the northernmost city dot.

"Fort Nelson. Head there. It'll be the last populated spot before we head even farther north."

She folded the map so their path could be easily read. Then she handed it back to Quinn.

He looked at it, then nodded. "Okay, now I can see where we need to go."

"You're welcome."

"I didn't say thank you."

"Yeah, but I know you wanted to and you were just being shy about it."

He laughed. "Oh, and you're so sure of what I want?"

It was an old argument and she wondered if he realized he'd settled comfortably into it. As she met his gaze, she toed off her shoes and put her feet up on the dash. "For some things, yup."

His eyes darkened as he took in her bare feet, then his gaze traveled the length of her leg up to her shoulders, then to her face. His longing for her was plain. She just wondered if he planned to do anything about it.

He shifted on the seat, clearly uncomfortable, then put his focus back on the road. The moment ended. "Settle in, because it's going to be a long haul. Twelve hours, at least, especially since we have to stay off the main roads."

Daeva cracked the window, letting in a warm breeze. She lifted her face to it as it fluttered over her skin. "Hey, I've been to hell, remember? I can endure anything."

Chapter 15

As Quinn drove he couldn't help but sneak looks at Daeva every once in a while. She was an easy woman to look at but his interest went beyond her physical appearance. He was starting to see the true person inside. And for the first time in years he questioned whether he had made a mistake when he'd exorcised her to hell without getting the whole story first. Would he have listened, though?

After two hours of his occasional glances, she turned and met his gaze directly. "Is there something you want to say?"

"No." He put his eyes back on the road.

"Quinn, I know you'll hate hearing it, but I know you pretty well and you definitely have something on your mind."

He sighed. "I don't hate it, exactly. It's just…"

"That I'm a demon and you're an exorcist, and like oil and water we don't mix?"

"No, I was going to say, that it's embarrassing to have someone know you so…"

"Intimately?"

He nodded. "Yeah."

"Well, technically we were together for three years."

"I know."

That had her gaping and it made him smile.

"So you admit it? You're not denying that I was the woman you were with?"

He shook his head. He was tired of denying it. It was exhausting fighting with the inevitable. "No, I'm not denying it."

She smirked. "Well, that's at least some progress. Maybe there is hope that you'll actually apologize to me for sending me back to hell."

He'd opened his mouth to do just that when he caught something in the rearview mirror. The local law.

"Shit. We've got company."

Daeva whipped around to look out the back window. "Do you think they made us?"

Before he could answer, the blue-and-red lights flashed on.

"Looks like we have our answer."

"What are you going to do?"

"Well, I'm definitely not going to pull over."

Daeva's fingers glowed. "I could blast him."

"Yeah and your little trick will be recorded on his dash cam for the whole world to see."

"We don't have many options, Quinn. Maybe humanity should know about demons."

"No blasting. Not unless absolutely necessary."

"I wasn't going to hurt him, just slow him down."

He sped up a little. The RCMP car following close behind, its light flashing incessantly.

"Can you aim for the tires? Melt them or something?"

"I can certainly try."

She rolled down the window and shimmied her body outside, so she was hanging half in and half out. "Keep the truck straight. I don't want to miss."

A booming voice came from the police car's speaker. "Please get back in the vehicle."

Canadians were so polite, Quinn thought.

Keeping the wheels straight, Quinn watched in the rearview mirror as Daeva launched a glowing ball of fire at the car behind them. The burning sphere hit the front right tire. It was a perfect shot.

Even from the distance, Quinn could see the surprise on the officer's face as the vehicle careened to the right, no longer supported by a tire. That tire was now a puddle of rubber stuck to the road. Before the vehicle flipped, the officer managed to get it stopped in the ditch.

"Nice shot," Quinn said, then put his attention back onto the road in front of them.

As they came over the rise, it was obvious they were far from safe.

Three more RCMP cars, lights on, blocked the road ahead. Three officers stood behind the hoods, weapons raised.

"I'm going to take a giant leap here and say this is about more than a stolen truck," Daeva said, even as her fingertips sparked with newly developed fire.

"You think?" Quinn slowed the truck, different scenarios racing through his head. None of them ended well.

"What do you want to do?"

He scanned the surroundings. Fortunately they were the only civilians on the long, straight stretch of road. Last thing he wanted was to get a bunch of innocent bystanders involved in this mess. Trees and farmland stretched out from the road like a green-and-yellow blanket.

"Hang on." Cranking the wheel to the left, Quinn took the truck off the road, bouncing across the ditch and into a patch of mustard plants. He gunned it and ploughed through a barbed-wire fence. As he drove across the field, he glanced in the rearview mirror to see two of the three cars giving chase. Although they weren't four-by-fours, they were catching up.

"We won't outrun them." Daeva pointed to a line of trees to the right. "Go there. We can get away from them on foot. Plus, it's getting dark and I'm the only one who can see in the dark. We'll have the advantage."

Quinn did as she suggested and jerked the wheel to the right so they were barreling toward a copse of pine trees. He stepped on the gas, pushing the truck past its limits. He could hear the engine whine, struggling to keep them at this speed. Then the right tire hit a buried tree stump hard, sending the truck tilting to the left.

To keep them upright, he turned the wheel and stepped on the brake. The tail end of the truck swung to the left and smashed into a tree trunk just outside the forest.

Knocked astray, Quinn hit his head against the side window. It was hard enough to crack the glass and send a jolt through his head. Pain exploded behind his left eye.

But he didn't have time to coddle himself before Daeva was yanking him out of the cab. "Come on!"

At first he was dizzy, a bit disoriented, but Daeva's constant pushing and prodding snapped him out of it.

"We need to get the gear."

She led him to the truck bed, then jumped in and tossed a full backpack at him. He caught it, and hooked it over his shoulder just as she jumped out with the other strapped to her shoulders. Together, they dashed into the trees as the two police cars stopped nearby.

Without looking back, Quinn ran, dodging broken tree stumps and jumping over fallen logs. Dusk had settled in, casting an eerie glow through the trees. Soon it would be difficult for him to see well. He glanced at Daeva who was in step with him, leaping and avoiding obstacles easily.

"You lead," he called to her.

With a quick nod, she moved in front of him, setting a pace that was quick and sprightly. He hoped he could keep up. It would do them no good if he lagged behind or, God forbid, fell on his face.

As Daeva led them deeper into the forest, he risked a glance over his shoulder to see if they were being followed by the RCMP officers. He sighed with relief when he couldn't see any movement behind them. But that didn't necessarily mean they had gotten away or were safe. They had to push it hard and long before they could take a breather. He had no doubt that it wasn't just the police chasing them. The pursuit was Cabal or demon motivated, just as it had been back at the border. They were being tracked by unnatural means.

He didn't know how long they'd been running before the light completely disappeared, but it wasn't too long. His head still throbbed, which didn't help his eyesight any. It was more instinct than anything else that saved him from plowing into a rotting tree leaning sideways. He dodged it, his shoulder brushing the bark, and kept going.

Daeva was a good five feet in front of him. But he was having trouble focusing on her. Fortunately she slowed a little when she came out into a clearing. Maybe they could stop a moment so he could have a quick drink of water. His lungs burned with exertion.

Just as he rushed into the clearing, Daeva was turning toward him, her hand thrust out. He knew she meant for him to stop, but it was too late. Momentum took him forward and he tripped and rolled down the incline to the stream below them.

"Quinn!"

Her voice followed him down into the icy water. It was as if a lightning bolt zapped his system when he landed face-first. Instinctually he pushed up with his hands and knees to get his face out. The stream wasn't very deep so he was able to get to his feet easily. But he was soaked right through and already starting to shiver from the chill in the air.

Daeva was beside him in a minute, boots in the water, helping him out. "Are you hurt?" Her gaze searched his face, then his body, looking for injuries.

"I'm okay. Just wet and cold."

"We have to keep going. I don't think we are far enough yet."

He nodded, knowing she was right. "Go. I'll follow."

"Are you sure?"

"Yeah. What else can we do? It's not like you can carry me." He meant it as a joke, but the way she was eyeing him made him nervous. "Hell, no."

"Don't be a baby. I won't tell anyone. It'll be our little secret." Her voice was even, but he caught the little smirk on her lips.

"Daeva, I swear I'll…"

She put her hand up. "Okay. Okay." She smiled. "You can't say I didn't care enough to suggest it." She wiped a hand over his face, brushing the wet hair from his eyes. "Just a little farther and we'll be able to rest."

She turned on her boot heel and crossed the stream to the other side. After adjusting his pack, Quinn followed her back into the trees, cold, wet but a little lighter inside. Her touch still tingled on his skin.

Chapter 16

They ran for another two hours but Daeva could see that Quinn couldn't keep up much longer. Even as he ran, she could see his body shaking with the cold that had probably crept to his bones. They needed to stop, make camp, and get him warm or he'd become hypothermic.

Over the next rise, she stopped in a small clearing. Bending over, she took in some deep breaths, curious that her body seemed to need them all of a sudden. Quinn stopped beside her, trying to do the same, but his chattering teeth impeded him.

"Why are we stopping?" he stammered.

She dumped her pack and dug through it for the small tent. "Because you're going to catch pneumonia or worse if we don't."

He didn't argue with her as she quickly put the tent together, which was a testament to how serious the situation was. And the fact that he knew not to disagree.

Once the tent was up, she pulled out a down-filled sleeping bag. "Strip."

"What?"

"Take off your clothes. They're wet and you need to get dry."

She unzipped the tent and shoved the sleeping bag inside. When she stood back up, he was pulling off his shirt, his hands shaking violently.

"Get in the tent and take the rest off. I'll start a fire and dry your clothes out."

Without a word, he crawled into the tent. Two minutes later, his wet jeans, socks and shorts came flying out. She found a branch to hang them on and proceeded to build a small fire beneath.

As she broke twigs apart and gathered moss and dry leaves together in a pile, she tried not to think about Quinn naked in the tent. Picturing his body, especially with no clothes on, never failed to ignite a fire deep inside her belly. Quinn was exquisitely crafted, with long, lean limbs, washboard abs, a strong, smooth chest and powerful shoulders. She loved big shoulders on a man. They were something substantial to sink her teeth into.

She shook the thought from her mind and concentrated on lighting the fire. She struck a match and held it to the dry moss and leaves. It smoldered and smoked but didn't ignite. She tried again, still no flames. Putting the matches aside she rubbed her right thumb and finger together. Soon, an orange glow emitted from her skin. She built a tiny sphere of red fire and rolled it into the kindling she'd gathered. In an instant, the leaves caught fire. A few seconds later, the twigs glowed, then flames licked upward. She sat bigger pieces of wood on the flames until she had a good fire going that wasn't going to go out anytime soon.

With that task completed, she turned toward the tent and wondered how Quinn was faring. Crouching, she unzipped the tent and stuck her head in.

"How are you doing?"

He didn't need to answer; she could see he couldn't talk because he was shaking so badly.

"Jesus, Quinn."

She crawled all the way in, took off her boots, then zipped up the tent flap. Quinn stared at her wide-eyed as she opened his sleeping bag.

"What the hell are you doing?"

"Getting you warm. Now shove over."

He did and she slid in next to him, zipping the bag so they were pressed right up against each other. Daeva wrapped her arms around his cold, shivering body and pressed herself into his back. She knew he wanted to protest, but she sensed her warmth was already seeping into him and he couldn't deny what his body needed.

"Relax," she said into his ear. "I'm not going to take advantage of you or anything." She nearly chuckled when she felt him relax.

Daeva spread her hands over his bare chest and pulled him tighter to her. His body should've been warming more quickly, but she feared her normal body heat wasn't enough. He was still shivering, his teeth chattering together loud enough to be heard outside the tent. She needed to do something extreme, something that Quinn wasn't going to like at all.

Lowering one of her hands to his stomach, she clamped her eyes shut and concentrated. She focused on the demon fire inside, and instead of making fire on her fingertips she focused on the heat she could create. Within seconds her skin flushed, heat rising to the surface in fiery waves.

Quinn squirmed against her. "Daeva," he whined. "What are you doing?"

"What needs to be done. Don't think about it and just accept it for once."

The heat increased in the sleeping bag and in the tent. It swelled quickly, causing Daeva to sweat. She wondered how upset he'd be if she stripped off her own clothes. Another five minutes of concentrating her fire, and Quinn's body stopped shaking.

"Better?" she asked.

He nodded.

She started to move her hands but he captured them with his own.

"Thank you, Daeva."

She smiled at the sincerity in his voice. Maybe they could finally overcome their past and become friends. To hope for more than that was beyond foolish. Quinn held on to his black-and-white morality too tightly.

"You're welcome," she murmured, then pressed a quick kiss to the back of his shoulder. She pulled her hands out from under his.

To do anything else would be wrong. Although she wanted to keep touching him, to feel all of him, she knew it was the wrong time, wrong place. Quinn would never forgive her if she pressed him further. Even though she was sure he would gladly welcome her advances, she knew he would berate himself afterward. If they ever gave in to their desires, desire she knew Quinn felt as well, she didn't want any regrets on either side.

She knew he wanted her, but wasn't sure if he even liked her.

Before she could change her mind, she quickly unzipped the bag, slid out and did it up again. Besides, Quinn needed sleep if he was to fully heal. They still had a long journey ahead of them.

She brushed a hand over his hair. "Go to sleep, Quinn. I'll set up wards and keep watch." Before she could see the answering longing in his eyes, she crawled out of the tent.

Chapter 17

Quinn rolled over to watch her zip up the flap on the tent. Earlier he'd nearly turned and asked her to stay with him. Her touch had done more than just warm his body—it had ignited something deep inside him. Something hot and primal.

There was no doubt that physically she turned him on in all kinds of ways. Her eyes, her body, her voice even sent ripples of desire through him constantly. It was his mind and possibly his heart that stopped him from acting on those impulses. His reservations definitely stemmed from their past history, but no longer did he deny that Daeva had been the woman he'd fallen in love with. He understood now that she'd just been in a different shell. A different package. But he could see that she was definitely the same person, although three years would definitely change a person, even a demon.

And that was what gave him pause. Knowingly falling for a demon was not something he wanted to deal with. He had enough on his plate as it was.

Yawning, Quinn pulled the sleeping bag tighter around his body and shut his eyes. He was going to need all his strength to deal with what was to come. Nothing was going to be safe. Certainly not with Daeva involved.

Quinn didn't know what time it was when he climbed out of the tent, but by the pinkening of the sky he could see through the tree canopy, it was early in the morning. He'd brought the sleeping bag out with him since he was still naked.

He didn't see Daeva when he looked around. He peered into the surrounding trees but didn't spy her red hair anywhere. The fire was still going, so she was likely somewhere close.

His clothes hung on a branch above the smoking coals. He hopped over to them. Fortunately, they were dry. Grabbing the shorts he quickly shucked the sleeping bag and stepped into them. He pulled on his pants, socks and shirt.

The snap of a branch made him turn just in time to see Daeva standing nearby, a container of something in her hand. She gave him a wide, cheesy grin. Obviously, she'd been there to witness him put his clothes on.

He shook his head. "Did you just watch me get dressed?"

"Yup. I thought about disturbing you, but you looked really cold, so I thought it better to wait until you were completely dressed."

That made him laugh as he plopped down on the sleeping bag and pulled on his boots. "Where did you go?" he asked as he tied his laces.

She showed him what was in the container. Plump, red raspberries. "Went to go pick some. Thought it would be a nice complement to the freeze-dried crap we have."

He took a handful and popped them into his

mouth. They were sweet and juicy. "Did you stay out here the whole time I slept?"

She nodded, eating some berries herself.

"Did you get any sleep?"

"Nah. I walked around, did some pull-ups on that branch there." She pointed to a thick tree branch about seven feet up. "I sang campfire songs to myself, then made some stick people."

He glanced down at the fire and spied a bunch of odd looking stick figures made from acorns and twigs and leaves. Surprised, he looked back at Daeva.

She shrugged. "What? I had to keep my hands and mind busy."

Not commenting, he crouched and rolled up the sleeping bag tightly. "We need to move on. Do you think the road is safe to travel?"

She offered him the last of the fruit, then said, "To be honest, no. I think every cop will be on the lookout for us."

"We can't hike the rest of the way. It'll take us more days than I'd like to think about."

"Hitchhike?"

He shook his head. "No one's going to pick us up. Maybe you on your own, but definitely not me. And we still have to watch out for cops."

"Then what?"

"I don't know." He kicked at the bedroll, frustrated. They seemed to be at a dead end. He could really see only one option and that was to keep to the trees as much as possible and hike it up north. Maybe they'd find a ride in the next town and maybe they wouldn't. Right now it didn't look too promising, not with the RCMP looking for them.

"I might have a solution," Daeva offered.

Quinn looked at her. "What?"

"You're not going to like it."

"I don't like the thought of hiking for days so you might as well hit me with it."

"Teleportation."

"Come again? I don't think I heard you right."

"I know a spell that could teleport us from here to Fort Nelson."

"Demon magic?"

She nodded. "I imagine you hate demon magic, but it's an option."

He sighed, rubbing a hand over his face, scrubbing away the fatigue. "How far would it take us?"

"I could get us close to where we need to be."

"Why didn't you mention this before now?"

She dropped her gaze to the ground and kicked at the debris on the forest floor. "Because it's not a spell I like doing. And it has its price." She glanced up and he saw a fierceness in her eyes.

He watched her for a long moment, taking her in, considering her. Trusting her. Then he said, "What do you need to get it done?"

"Your chalk, something purple, and blood."

"How much blood?"

She hesitated then said, "Enough to make a mess."

A half hour later, Daeva had finished chalking a series of symbols on a nearby tree trunk in a pentagram pattern. He recognized a couple, one for travel, the other for door, but the others he didn't know. And probably didn't want to know.

He studied them a minute longer, then studied her. She was nervous. He could see it in the way her hand trembled while she drew the symbols. She also tugged at her hair. It was a gesture he recognized from when they'd been together.

"Are you okay?" he asked, worried about her, worried about the spell she was going to cast.

He was concerned about what teleportation would do to him, traveling through a portal not made for human physiology. How would he come out on the other end? With his arm attached to his head?

She glanced at him, pulled at the strand of her hair again. Those few strands came out with her frequent tugging. Surprised, she looked at them then let them drift down to the forest floor.

"I'm good."

But he could plainly see she wasn't. She really looked afraid.

"Do you have the something purple?"

He handed her a small, square piece of cloth. He'd used it to clean his knives over the years. It had been his father's. She took it, nodding to him, likely knowing its significance and folded it to slip into her pocket.

"Now we need blood. Know how to make a snare?"

After several failed attempts, they managed to snare a young rabbit. It looked pretty scrawny but it didn't matter—it wasn't the meat they needed.

Daeva was quick and deft with the blade. Most women would be squeamish about gutting an animal but he supposed Daeva wasn't like most women. Or any woman for that matter.

She used what she needed, painting the blood onto the tree with her fingers. Once that was done, she reached into her pocket, took out the purple fabric and stuck it to the tree with the knife. When she was finished, she took a step back and reached with her hand for Quinn.

"Take my hand and hold on tight. Do not let go of me for any reason. Understand?"

He nodded, swallowing the lump of fear lodged in his throat. "What about our gear?"

"I can't bring it through. Just you and me." She squeezed his hand. "Are you ready for this?"

"No."

"Shut your eyes and don't open them." She gave him a smile. "Trust me. I won't let anything happen to you."

With that she spread out the fingers of her other hand and pressed them to the tree trunk, each fingertip touching a symbol.

"Eo ire itum."

The air around him vibrated, then everything went dark.

It was as if he was being sucked through a straw by some huge, cosmic mouth. Quinn felt pulled on and yanked and pushed and manipulated through a series of narrow twisty passages. He tried not to think about it and just concentrated on the feel of Daeva's hand in his own.

The air they whizzed through was ice cold, then sweltering, then ice cold again, with each corner they twisted around. It took all Quinn had not to open his eyes. He suspected he didn't want to know exactly what they were moving through. His skin itched and burned from whatever tainted air touched him. Once they were through, he would find a way to have a shower.

As they continued being towed through the ether by some unseen force, Quinn couldn't keep his eyes closed any longer. His curiosity won out over his fear and he risked a look.

What he saw filled him with awe, not fear.

It was almost as if they were standing still with time and space whizzing by them on either side at lightning speed. He only got fleeting glimpses of things but he sensed he and Daeva weren't just moving through this reality but several of them at once. Realities he couldn't even begin to comprehend. It was amazing. He wondered if demons appreciated having this kind of knowledge and access to other worlds. What power that was to possess. His stomach churned watching it all go by.

Curious as to Daeva's comment on keeping his eyes closed, he turned her way and was dumbstruck by her appearance. He realized now why she'd told him to close his eyes. It wasn't the worlds they were spinning through that she thought would frighten him, but her.

She turned and met his gaze, her eyes as black and liquid as ink. "I told you not to look." Her voice was deep and guttural, but not entirely unpleasant.

Her hair swept around as if it were licks of fire, alive and aware. Her already pale skin glowed like blue flame. It was both alien and beautiful, and it made him want to reach out and run his fingertips along her arms and shoulders to feel the heat he was sure she was generating.

"Close your eyes, Quinn, don't look at me like this."

When she spoke he spied the tiny points of fangs in her mouth. For some that might have instilled fear but not for Quinn.

He thought she was exquisite in all her foreignness.

"You're beautiful, Daeva."

Her eyes widened in disbelief at that. It made him sad to see it. That she thought her true form so ugly she'd hidden it from him all along. Although he'd given her every reason to do so. He'd only shown her his prejudice against demons.

Then everything went black again, as if a shutter had snapped shut on his eyes.

And they appeared suddenly on a gravel road in the middle of a thick grouping of evergreen trees.

Quinn stumbled a little from the jarring vertigo caused by their sudden arrival but he succeeded in keeping on his feet. He looked over at Daeva just as she let go of his hand. She buckled like a rag doll. He caught her before she could hit the ground and laid her gently down on the grass beside the road. Her hair stuck to her sweat-slicked face. He brushed it off her forehead. She was burning up with a fever.

He now understood when she said there'd be a price to pay. This was it. Her. She was the price.

"Daeva, what can I do? What do you need?"

She blinked up at him, her pupils dilated. He wasn't even sure she was focusing on him. Smiling, she reached up with her hand and stroked it down his cheek.

"Blackbird," she murmured. Then her hand fell limp to her side and she passed out.

Quinn tried to revive her but it was no use. She was out. He stroked her face, unsure what to do for her. He knew he couldn't leave her out here; he had to get her somewhere safe and warm. A place he could nurse her back to health.

Tucking his hand under her legs, he lifted her into his arms and started down the road. Hopefully he'd come across a house, or a vehicle would come across him.

He'd walked for about an hour before his legs and arms started to feel the strain of carrying her. It wouldn't be long before he had to set her down for a rest. To make matters even worse, the gray clouds that had been swirling overhead opened up and hard, cold rain pounded down on them.

Nearing his breaking point, Quinn jostled Daeva in his arms to get a better grip on her and that's when he spotted a small sign in the tall grass near the branching of a dirt driveway. It read Blackbird Lodge. Quinn nearly wept with joy.

The lodge was a small log cabin that had seen

better days. But there was a light in the window, so someone had to be home. Quinn carried Daeva up the steps to the front deck and knocked on the door.

Slowly the door opened and a woman, maybe a little older than he, with long, silky, black hair peered out. "Yes?"

"I think you can help me."

She glanced at Daeva, wet and limp in his arms. She pressed her fingers to Daeva's cheek and studied her face. "She is one of the fire people."

She dropped her hand and took a step to the side, clearing the doorway. "Bring her in."

Chapter 18

The dream was about one of her favorite days, and one of her last with Quinn.

Sunbeams pierced the fluttering curtains and played over Quinn's bare back as he lay on his stomach, face planted sideways into the mattress.

Daeva had always loved to trace the light's pattern on his skin with her fingertips as they lounged in bed on Sunday mornings. It had been her favorite day of the week. Neither of them had work to do or any other commitments. They would spend most of the day in and out of bed, being lazy, just enjoying the heck out of each other.

On one particular day, Daeva had decided to sneak out of the bed, go down to the market and pick up something special for lunch. They'd feasted earlier on a hearty meal of French toast and bacon, then made love until they both "fell asleep" again. Except Daeva rarely slept. So she would often just lie beside Quinn and watch him sleep.

She slowly swung her legs out of the bed and stood. Padding across the bedroom floor, she grabbed a tank top and shorts and left the room. After quickly dressing in the bathroom, she grabbed her wallet from the table and slid on a pair of sandals.

The market near their condo wasn't too busy, but she took her time browsing and bartering regardless. She loved the process and wondered how anyone could shop any other way. This was much more rewarding, for the buyer and the seller.

Carrying her paper bag of peppers, cilantro and freshly fried beignets, Daeva made her way back to the condo. She was going to make a taco salad with her Hot Pepper Salsa from

Hell recipe. It was her special recipe, something she'd literally picked up in hell. Klix had made it for her whenever she'd asked.

As she rounded the corner to their street, she paused. Someone was following her. Not just anyone but someone from the old homestead down below.

She turned in a circle, searching the street, especially the dark and secluded places, for her interested party. She spied the telltale flash of pointy green ears in an alleyway across the street. Squaring her shoulders she marched across the road and into the secluded alley.

She saw him crouched beside a green garbage can. He was camouflaged against it. If a person hadn't been specially looking for a four-foot goblin, they would certainly miss him.

"What are you doing here, Klix?" she asked him.

"I am worried about you, Mistress." His big opaque eyes regarded her openly.

"There is nothing to worry about. You can see I am perfectly well."

He tilted his shiny, bald, oblong head. "Your human puppet clothing suits you."

"Thank you." She glanced down the alley to

make sure they were still alone. "Now, what is the real reason for this unexpected visit?"

"There have been questions, Mistress."

"About what?"

"You. Your business topside."

"I'm on holiday. That's all they need to know."

"The exorcist, Mistress."

"What about him?"

His gaze shifted side to side nervously. "They ask about him. His importance to you."

"And what do you say?"

"Nothing. I say I don't know this exorcist. Don't know what they are talking about."

She nodded. "That's good, Klix. You are a trustworthy friend."

He brightened at that, his gnarled lips twitching into a kind of grin. Other demons treated Klix and his ilk like slaves, like servants, but Daeva had always considered him so much more. They were not dumb insignificant creatures. Most of the goblins Daeva knew were clever, fierce and loyal. And Klix was smarter than all of them put together. That's why she'd befriended him over a millennium ago. It was always wise to have a loyal friend in hell.

"But I fear they will not listen to me for long," he said. "I am not equal to them."

She nodded. "Yes, I fear that, as well."

She needed to be prepared for that inevitable day. The lords of hell would come for her eventually, but worst of all, they would come for Quinn. Because she loved him, they would take him from her to punish her for abandoning hell and the demon way. For trying to bury her demon roots and become something else. Something she'd always wanted to be—human. They would consider her a traitor and punish her as much as they could. Destroying the only man she'd ever love would be the perfect way.

She had to protect Quinn. But how? Maybe it was time for her to go back. Maybe only that way could she keep Quinn safe.

Daeva nodded to her little goblin friend. "You've done well, Klix. Thank you for your warning."

He bowed to her. "I will continue to keep the horde at bay but don't know for how much longer."

She gave him a small smile. "I know, and it is not your responsibility, Klix, to do so. It is mine. I will do what I must here."

"Be well, Mistress."

"Be well, Klix."

Then he took a step backward and vanished into the brick wall.

Daeva left the alley to return to the condo. She and Quinn needed to have a talk. Maybe today was the day to tell him the truth. She had to risk it, risk everything she'd worked for, to save his life.

When she arrived home, Quinn met her in the kitchen. He took the bags from her, putting them on the counter. "I was wondering where you went off to." He peeked in the bag. "What are you making?"

"Salsa for taco salad."

"Sounds scrumptious." He grabbed her around the waist, pulled her close and kissed her quickly on the mouth.

"Ah, Quinn, we need to talk about something."

He kissed her again, this time nibbling on her bottom lip. "Can it wait? Because we have a..."

Surprised, Daeva looked up just as another woman stepped into the kitchen.

"Ivy came for a visit," Quinn finished quickly.

Daeva smiled at Quinn's younger sister. "Hi, Ivy. Good to see you."

"Hey. I hope I'm not intruding."

Daeva could see the sadness in the girl's face. They had lost their father not that long ago, before she met Quinn, and she knew Ivy had been close to him.

"No problem. I can make more than enough for everyone."

Ivy smiled as Quinn kissed Daeva again. "And this is just one of the many reasons I love you."

He let her go, then opened the fridge to take out a couple of beers. He twisted the cap off one and handed it to Ivy. Daeva didn't drink beer.

"Come on, let's leave the culinary genius to go to work."

He guided Ivy out of the kitchen, winking at Daeva on the way out.

She leaned on the counter trying to steady herself. Tears threatened to well in her eyes. She would miss these kinds of days. These normal human days. But she knew without a doubt that she had to do something. Quinn was in danger. And, by default, so was Ivy. Just having her in their lives meant their days were numbered.

Daeva didn't want that on her conscience. She'd leave as soon as she could.

"Daeva?"

Slowly, she blinked open her eyes. The room was gloomy. There were no sunbeams playing across the bed. She licked her lips. They were dry and cracked. Blinking again, she turned her head to see Quinn sitting beside the bed on a wooden chair. He was holding her hand, stroking his thumb over her knuckles.

"What…what happened?"

"You passed out after we teleported. You've been out for fourteen hours."

She looked around, taking in the small wooden room. They were definitely in a log cabin; she could see the round logs of the wall.

"Where are we?"

"I didn't know what to do. You said 'Blackbird' before you passed out. So I brought you here."

"Where's here?"

"Blackbird Lodge."

She licked her lips again. Quinn brought a cup of water to her mouth and helped her drink.

"I was dreaming of before."

He gave her a little smile. "I know. You were talking in your sleep again."

"Oh." She was a little embarrassed, wondering exactly what she said out loud.

The bedroom door opened and a lean woman with long, black, braided hair came in. "Good. You're awake."

Daeva stared at her. "You are a Blackbird."

The woman nodded. "I am Leanne Blackbird."

"I knew your great-grandfather, William. I believe he left a map for me."

Chapter 19

An hour later, they were sitting in Leanne Blackbird's kitchen. Quinn had helped Daeva out of the bed and to the table. She'd managed to eat some soup and fresh bread, and he thought her coloring was coming back. She'd been as pale as death when she'd been unconscious, gray almost, her lips a tinge of blue. The thought of her not waking had tied his guts in knots. They were a little less knotted now, but he was still worried about her. More than he'd first realized.

He'd always thought demons were indestructible, unbreakable, but just looking at Daeva told him that was far from the truth.

Leanne had insisted that Daeva eat before she would bring her the map. Quinn had been surprised there had even been a map, but realized he shouldn't have been surprised by anything, especially when it came to Daeva. She had told him that she'd had help hiding the chest over one hundred years ago. He guessed he knew who that help had been—William Blackbird, Leanne's great-grandfather.

What surprised him the most was Leanne's lack of surprise. She'd known Daeva was a demon or fire person, and that Daeva had been well-enough acquainted with Leanne's great-grandfather to entrust him with something very important.

It had been obvious Leanne knew something about demons, because she'd known exactly what to do to make Daeva well.

For those fourteen hours, she'd helped Quinn break Daeva's fever with a combination of liquids and some concoction she brewed that she'd spread over Daeva's forehead, chest and back. It had smelled strongly of pine and eucalyptus. She'd also done some kind of ceremony around

Daeva's bed. It was in the Cree language, so Quinn couldn't understand it. All he knew was that it had worked.

Daeva's fever had broken and her skin had started taking on color again. Relief had surged through him at the sight of her cheeks flushing when he'd touched them.

Thoughts of her death had filled his mind. And when they had, the agony he felt was surprising. For a few days now, Quinn had been coming to terms with his feelings for Daeva. They weren't residual emotions for a woman long gone, but new feelings for this demon before him.

After clearing away the dishes, Leanne disappeared into what he assumed was her bedroom, then returned with a rolled-up paper, yellow with age.

She handed it to Daeva. "He must've known you would return one day."

"Have you looked at it?" Daeva asked.

Leanne shook her head. "My grandfather told me many stories when he passed it on to me, but I never wanted to know."

Daeva untied the leather binding around the

map and unrolled it, spreading it across the table. Quinn held the edges down for her.

It was obviously a map of the area, but it was old. The date scrawled on the frayed bottom edge was 1913. Over a hundred years ago. He looked at Daeva. She had been here then.

She met his gaze and gave him one of her trademark sassy smiles, knowing exactly what he was thinking. "I look good for being so old, hey?"

"You look barely twenty-five," he said, returning her smile.

"Oh, Quinn, you're such a charmer."

Leanne looked from him to her, then back, probably trying to figure them out. Hell, he couldn't even do that.

Daeva pointed to a small circle on the map and asked Leanne, "Do you know this place?"

Leanne leaned on the table and looked the map over. She nodded. "Yes, I think so. It's an old iron mine."

"Could you take us there?" Daeva asked.

"It's closed now, has been for decades. The roads are overgrown. There's nothing there."

"There *is* something there and I need to find it. Please, can you take us?"

Leanne didn't look at Daeva. Quinn could see the hesitation on her face. He didn't blame her. She had no idea what she could be getting into. Although they seemed safe right now, he knew the Cabal and quite possibly other demons wouldn't stop pursuing them. The chest was the key to more power than any of them could comprehend.

"We understand if you can't, Leanne. You've already done so much."

She looked at him and he saw more than hesitation in her dark brown eyes. He saw regret, maybe even resentment.

"I will take you."

"Are you sure?" Quinn asked. "We won't lie to you, it could be dangerous. There are others after the same thing we are."

"It is my duty as a Blackbird to do so." Leanne sighed, her hands fidgeting at her sides.

"What do you mean?"

Daeva answered, "There was a curse put on her family line a few hundred years ago."

He frowned. "What?"

Leanne gave him a sad half smile. "I never believed the stories. I'd always thought it was one of the old myths about the fire people." She looked at Daeva. "I didn't believe until I saw you on my porch. Then I knew it was my turn to fulfill the conditions of the family curse."

She turned to look out the kitchen window. "I will get our gear ready to go at first light." She turned and left the kitchen, opening the front door and exiting.

Quinn paced the room. "We shouldn't be asking her to do this. It's too dangerous. With the map we can find it ourselves."

"She's bound to this task, Quinn. She has to do it." Daeva stood, wobbled a little and had to brace herself against the tabletop.

"Can't you find the damn demon that cast the curse and have him remove it? Evil sonofabitch, doing something like that."

She pushed away from the table and moved toward the bathroom. "I'm going to have a shower. I feel like I've been living in these clothes for weeks."

He followed her, not content to let the conversation go. "Did you hear me, Daeva?"

"Yes," she hissed, "I heard you just fine. But there's nothing I can do about it."

He took her arm to stop her from entering

the bathroom. "You know the bastard that cast the curse, don't you?"

She braced a hand against the door frame and glared at him. "Yes, I know."

"Who was it?"

"Me." She put her hand on the door. "Now, if you'll excuse me, I stink, so I'd like to shower please."

Quinn slapped his hand on the door before she could close it. "What do you mean you put the curse on the family?"

"I'm a demon, aren't I? That's part of being a demon, enslaving a family to do your bidding."

"I can't believe it. It's so…"

"Evil?" She raised an eyebrow sardonically, but he saw the hurt in her eyes. "I am a demon, Quinn, or have you forgotten? I'd be surprised if you have."

"It's just, I thought…"

"What? You keep reminding me that I'm not human. I'm not sure why this is so surprising to you."

He looked at her, trying to figure her out. She sounded angry, but not necessarily at him. Just in general. Angry at the situation, maybe, or at herself.

"I know you're not the same person you were three years ago, Daeva. I think I know who you are."

"Well, if you're not going to volunteer to wash my back, then I really think this conversation is over."

After a long moment, Quinn removed his hand from the door and she shut it firmly in his face. He'd let her have her privacy for now, but she was gravely mistaken if she thought the conversation was over.

Chapter 20

Daeva stripped off her clothes and stepped thankfully into the shower stall. She cranked the tap all the way to Hot. It hurt when the scalding spray hit her, but only for a moment. Then it just melted gloriously into her skin and bones. Her muscles started to unknot under the blistering jet.

After being in the cold, on the run, and sleeping in uncomfortable positions for a couple of days, the hot, cleansing shower was like a little piece of utopia. She wished she could just stay in here and let the world move on without her, but she had to face her situation sooner or later. Just when she thought Quinn had stopped thinking of her as an evil demon and was regarding her and treating her as the woman he'd fallen in love with six years ago, he'd been reminded of her true nature.

She was born a demon and would always remain so. No matter what she did, he would now forever remember that she'd cursed someone. Well, enslaved a whole family line, really. It didn't matter that she'd only taken advantage of that curse once before, the time she'd buried the Chest of Sorrows inside an iron mine. A place no demon could see through or human could ever get to, to obtain it, especially if they didn't know where to look. She should've gotten extra brownie points for that. She'd saved the human race by burying it deep in the Earth.

Once she was thoroughly warmed through to the bone, she found shampoo in the corner caddy. It smelled of oranges. She glopped some in her palms and massaged it deeply into her scalp. The odor sent an invigorating shiver through her. She wished Quinn had volunteered to help her wash. His strong hands massaging her head, running through her hair, made her body quiver with need. It had been a long time since she'd had sex or any intimate contact with a man; the last time had been with Quinn. She wondered what he would say if he knew that. Would it make a difference to him?

Thinking about Quinn was making her dizzy, or it could've been the steam in the shower that made her light-headed. She took in some deep breaths, but it didn't help, so she reached up for the showerhead to keep her balance, but it was too late. She dropped to her knees, hitting her head on the shower stall.

There was a rush of cold air as the bathroom door opened. "Daeva? Are you all right?"

She didn't answer. Her tongue felt thick in her mouth. All she could manage was an undignified squeak. Quinn slid open the stall door and she fell forward into his arms before she could hit the hard tiled floor.

Not caring that he was getting wet, he reached up and turned off the water. Then he grabbed a large bath towel and wrapped her in it.

"Can you walk?"

She nodded, although she wasn't positive she could, really.

He helped her to her feet. Leaning heavily

on him, Daeva let Quinn guide her back to the guest bedroom. She'd never been this weak before, this vulnerable. And she hated it.

He lowered her onto the bed. "You obviously need more rest."

"Obviously," she mumbled.

He ran a hand over her wet hair. "You're not made of steel, Daeva. You can't go two hundred percent one hundred percent of the time. It's apt to take its toll. You said yourself that being bound to the Earth and to me diminished your powers."

"I know. It just sucks."

He chuckled at that. "Yeah, it does." His hand was still on her head. "Wait here. I'll be right back."

"Where else am I going to go?"

He left the room, then came back a few seconds later with another towel. He sat beside her on the bed, nudging her sideways with his leg. He picked up her wet wall of hair and settled it on the other towel.

"What are you doing?"

"Drying your hair. I don't have a comb but my fingers should do."

Touched, Daeva let Quinn comb his fingers

through her hair while squeezing the excess water from the strands. It was a tender thing to do. She'd never had anyone care for her like that. Even when they'd been together before, when she was masquerading as a human, he'd never offered to do that. Unexpectedly, tears formed in the corners of her eyes. But she didn't want him to see her so emotional, so weak.

"I want you to know," she started, her voice quavering a little, "that I did that curse a long time ago. I was different then."

"I realize that, Daeva."

"You do?"

"I mean, I've changed in the past five years, so it's easy to think that someone has changed in over two hundred years."

He continued to run his fingers through the wet strands of her hair. She let her head fall back a little, pure pleasure cascading over her like a warm blanket. She sighed happily.

"Feel good?"

"Oh, hell, yeah." She was hyperaware of his presence behind her and the fact that she was still only wearing a towel, was naked and wet underneath.

His hands paused; she sensed that he dropped

them to his sides. She glanced over her shoulder and saw the hesitation in his face, the uncertainty. The fear.

"Maybe you should get under the covers and get some more sleep."

"I'm not tired anymore."

She couldn't hide the fact that she wanted him. It was too tiring to constantly check her libido. She wanted Quinn in every way possible. Even when she was furious with him for being judge, jury and exorcist, she'd never stopped wanting.

He'd changed, too. He wasn't as trusting or easy-going, his heart had toughened a little, but she still saw the compassionate and caring man underneath his hardened exterior.

He stood with his hands fisted at his sides. "We both need rest. We still have a long journey ahead."

"Yeah, we do, which is why we should address this thing between us."

"What thing is that, exactly?"

She twisted around, her towel gaping up the length of her thigh. Quinn's eyes tracked the movement.

"The sexual tension."

His eyes darkened. "I think it's best we ignore it."

She reached for his hand. "Quinn, I want you. And I know you want me."

"Do you really think this is the best time or place?"

"It's the perfect time. We might not get another chance." She tugged him closer. "I don't want to lose this one chance, Quinn. I don't want to lose…" She couldn't finish her thought; it was too painful to speak out loud.

By the look in his eyes, she wasn't sure he could handle hearing that she still loved him.

He raised his other hand to her face. With just his fingertips he traced the line of her chin to her mouth. Cupped her cheek in his palm.

"You won't lose me."

"But don't you see? I will, one way or another, after we find the chest."

He didn't say anything, then, because he knew she spoke the truth. Instead, he ran a hand over her hair.

"Come on. Get under the covers. You need the rest."

She did as he asked and slid under the covers, the towel still wrapped around her. "Will you stay with me until I fall asleep?"

He nodded and crawled onto the bed behind her. He wrapped an arm over her on top of the covers and pulled her close.

Sighing, Daeva closed her eyes. Exhaustion was taking its toll on her and she was finding it difficult to stay lucid. The warmth of Quinn's body and the way he stroked her hair was comforting, lulling her to sleep. When she finally succumbed to it, it was with his scent in her nose and the press of his lips on her shoulder.

Chapter 21

It wasn't quite dawn when Daeva slid quietly from the bed and dressed in the clothes Leanne had given her. After putting her hair up in a high ponytail, she silently padded out of the room, shutting the door behind her. She didn't want to wake Quinn. He needed the rest, both his body and mind.

He'd held her until she fell asleep. But she wasn't out for long. Daeva tried to go back under but she had too much on her mind. Although her body was exhausted from the teleportation, she still couldn't sleep. There was too much to do.

Quinn had been in a deep sleep, by the looks of him. So she'd covered him with the blanket then slid out from under his arm.

The cabin was dark but she knew that Leanne was already awake and waiting because there was a fresh pot of coffee brewed. Daeva poured a cup, and as she sipped it, she glanced out the kitchen window to the predawn glow. That was when she spotted Leanne outside, sitting cross-legged on a blanket spread out on the deck. Her eyes were closed.

As if sensing Daeva's gaze, her eyes opened and she looked right at her. Daeva could see the latent power in the Cree woman. She possessed more strength than she probably even knew.

A couple of minutes later, the front door opened and Leanne came back in, the colorful blanket draped over her arm.

"You are up early," Leanne said as she put the blanket into an old painted wooden trunk.

"I don't need much sleep."

"Neither do I." Leanne came over to the coffeemaker and poured a cup, liberally adding sugar. She took her coffee and sat at the table. Daeva joined her.

They drank in silence. Daeva watched the woman over the rim of her cup. She knew Leanne wanted to ask her something and was gathering the nerve to do it.

"You are the demon that cursed my line, aren't you?"

"Yes."

"Why?"

"Out of arrogance, I suppose." Daeva ran her finger over the rim of the cup. "Your ancestor was a great warrior but he wanted more power. He called upon the dark forces to help him in his quest. He was lucky that it was me that answered the call and not another more vicious demon." She watched Leanne flinch at that. "He demanded my allegiance to help him become chief. I gave it to him, but told him his entire lineage would forever be enslaved to me. He readily agreed. He didn't even think about it." She picked up the coffee and drank to wet her suddenly dry throat. "I only used the curse once, with your great-grandfather, to help me hide something, a most important and dangerous artifact. And now, of course you, to help me find it."

The Cree woman nodded. "The stories I have heard over the years have changed somewhat."

Daeva smiled. "Of course they did. No one wants to believe that their ancestor was a greedy, selfish, power-hungry jerk."

Leanne sighed. "I will help you find what you seek."

"When we are done, I promise you I will lift the curse so that the rest of your family is free from it."

Leanne nodded. "Thank you."

There was a long pause, then a voice came from the corner. "Good morning."

Both women turned as Quinn stepped into the kitchen. Daeva suspected he'd heard their entire conversation.

As he passed her to get some coffee, he ran his hand over her head. He poured a cup and leaned against the counter with it.

"How long will it take us to get where we need to go?"

"It is an hour drive, then we have to hike the rest of the way in."

"How far?" he asked.

"About sixteen miles."

"That's a long haul."

Leanne nodded. "We won't make it today. We'll have to make camp and not wander the area at night. There are bears and cougars around."

"We might run into other trouble," he said.

"There's no 'might' about it." Daeva lifted her cup. "The Cabal will show."

Leanne nodded. "I have protection."

The door opened and a tall young man with the same long black hair and dark eyes as Leanne came in. He carried a rifle in his big hands.

He glanced at Quinn, then at Daeva, his distrust and distaste evident in the way he frowned.

Leanne stood and greeted him with a hug and kiss on his cheek. "This is my son, Billy."

Quinn nodded to him, but Billy ignored the gesture. It was obvious his only concern was for his mother. He took her arm and guided her into the living room. They also spoke in Cree, but Daeva understood them, anyway.

"Let me come with you," Billy pleaded. "You can't trust these people."

"No, Billy, you must stay here. I can take care of myself. I am not useless."

"I didn't say that, but it is dangerous, especially with that fire hag."

Daeva snorted. "Hey, I resent that. I'm not even close to being a hag."

Leanne looked surprised. "You understand Cree?"

Daeva smiled, but without humor. "I understand all languages. The beauty of being from hell, I suppose. It's multicultural."

Billy came into the kitchen, his hands fisted. He looked ready to pummel her. She could feel the fury rising off him.

"Leave this house, demon. You are not welcome."

Daeva stood, not liking being threatened while she sat. "Your mother welcomed me. This is her home, is it not?"

He went to speak again, but his mother was there beside him, calming him with her hand on his shoulder. "It is okay, Billy. I will be safe. You don't have to worry."

He turned to her, still angry. Daeva could tell he wanted to say so much more, but he had respect for his mother so he bit his tongue.

"Take the GPS tracker, so I know where you are."

"If it will ease your mind, son."

He nodded, then bent to kiss Leanne on the cheek. He spoke in Cree again. "I love you, Mother."

"And I you. I will see you soon."

With that, he was gone, leaving the rifle in his mother's capable hands.

"My son worries too much."

Daeva smiled at her. "He loves his mother. There is nothing wrong with that."

"No, there isn't." Leanne returned the smile. "I will meet you out back and we will grab the gear we'll need." She left them in the kitchen to prepare for their trip.

Daeva set her empty cup in the sink. Quinn reached for her hand.

"He said those things because he doesn't know you. The real you."

"He has the right to be upset. We're putting his mother at great risk. Because of something I did centuries ago."

"Yeah, but we'll keep her safe. She'll be all right."

Daeva nodded but with no real conviction. Ever since she'd woken, a sense of impending

doom had filled her gut. She knew that feeling, had had it before. It meant someone was
going to die.

Chapter 22

As they packed Leanne's Range Rover with their gear and supplies, Daeva glanced up at the sky and shivered. The gray clouds of earlier had now turned an ominous, swirling slate black.

Quinn came to stand beside her at the back of the vehicle. "I definitely don't like the looks of that sky."

"Me either."

A bolt of lightning pierced the black clouds, making them both flinch. It was followed by a clap of thunder that shook the Range Rover.

Leanne shut the hatch on the vehicle. "This is

not good weather for our journey. We're going to have to postpone."

As if to punctuate her statement, the heavens opened up and spewed rain and hailstones the size of golf balls onto their heads.

"I'm putting the Rover back into the garage." Leanne jumped into the front seat.

As she pulled it forward into the safety of the car port, Daeva and Quinn ran to the safety of the cabin's covered porch.

They watched in horror as the ground, the trees and surrounding buildings were assaulted by the substantially sized balls of ice. It was so loud that Daeva couldn't hear anything above it. Leanne was pelted hard as she ran from the garage to the cabin. Pieces of ice hung off the tips of her braided hair.

"I haven't seen a storm like this in decades," she confessed.

"Maybe it's a sign," Quinn said.

Although Daeva suspected he was joking, she heard the uncertainty in his voice. Maybe it *was* a sign. But she had no delusions that it was sent by heaven.

She searched the neighboring forest. Were

they alone? Or did they have company of the sorcerer kind?

"We should get inside," Leanne said, as hailstones slammed onto the porch right next to her boot. She opened the door and went in. Daeva and Quinn followed her lead.

It was almost deafening inside as the hail pounded against the cabin's wooden and tin exterior. Then the wind picked up, battering the ice against the walls and windows. A sharp crack came from Leanne's bedroom.

"Sounds like a window," Daeva said, pointing to the room.

All three of them rushed in to see an orange-sized hailstone on the floor. Splinters of glass were spread across the floor.

Cursing, Leanne gestured to Quinn. "There's wood, a hammer and some nails just outside on the porch."

He turned and rushed out of the room to retrieve them.

"What can I do?" Daeva asked.

"There's a broom in the kitchen."

Daeva ran out to get it, easily finding it hanging on a peg near the garbage. She brought the broom and dustpan back to the bedroom. She helped Leanne sweep up the glass as Quinn returned with two planks of wood and the hammer and nails.

The wind whipped more rain and ice into the room before Quinn could board it up. Just as he finished pounding in the last nail, the lights flickered then went out.

"Is this normal?" Quinn asked, obviously feeling the same unease Daeva felt.

"We've had storms like this before during the summer." Leanne stared at Daeva. "Is there something I should know?"

"We have sorcerers after us. So it's possible this could be one of their spells."

"This is pretty powerful magic, if it is."

"I agree," Daeva said. "I'm not sure if it's them at all. Could be just Mother Nature doing her damnedest to destroy stuff."

"What do you want to do?" Quinn asked.

He looked nervous. Daeva could see his hands fidgeting at his sides. One of the benefits of night vision was seeing all the things people generally want to keep hidden, especially in the dark.

"Well, we're no good just standing here." Leanne walked out of the bedroom. Daeva and

Quinn followed her into the living room. "We'll need light and heat."

She settled some kindling in the fireplace and lit a match, holding it down to the wood. The flame went out without taking. Frustrated, she lit another match.

"Here, let me." Daeva nudged her aside, crouching next to the hearth. She rubbed two fingers together. At first, nothing happened. A ball of fear rolled in her stomach. Was she losing her powers?

Trying not to appear worried, she kept rubbing her fingers together. Harder. Faster. Until finally a spark formed, then more, and she had a small orb of fire that she dropped into the middle of the kindling. The wood sparked and smoked until it flickered with flames.

She let out the breath she'd been holding, then set a few larger logs onto the popping fire. When she stood and turned, Quinn was watching her intently, his brow furrowed.

She gave him a small smile. "No sweat."

But she didn't think he believed her by the way he kept watching her.

"Well, all we can do now is hunker down and wait it out." Leanne picked up the gun her son had left her and carried it into the kitchen. "Anyone want a drink? I'm having a drink." She opened the cupboard and took out a bottle of Scotch.

"Sounds like a helluva idea." Daeva joined her in the kitchen and took three short glasses down from the shelf.

Leanne filled each glass, then set the bottle down on the table in front of the fire. She plucked one glass up and lifted it in salute.

They all drank. Then Leanne filled up their glasses again.

"If there was any time to get drunk, I think it's now." Leanne chugged back the second drink.

Daeva cheered her with her own glass. "Hear, hear. I've been wanting to get drunk from the moment I arrived topside."

"Come, sit, and tell me what it's like to be a demon."

Leanne took a seat in the overstuffed chair near the fireplace. Daeva slid onto the sofa. Quinn sat next to her. He had yet to say anything and just watched her. She wondered if he, too, wanted to know what it was like to be a demon. Was he looking for some insight?

She gave him a small smile, and he set his hand on her leg and squeezed it reassuringly. She liked that he was near. It made her feel safe. Something she didn't normally feel on a daily basis.

"It's not as fun as you'd think." She laughed, but without any real humor.

Leanne frowned at her. "I didn't think it would be fun at all."

"It isn't. But you can't choose how you are born or what you are born into."

"No, you can't." Leanne poured more whiskey into her glass. "But you must learn to accept the things you can't change."

They were all silent for a few minutes, then Daeva started to tell her tale. Leanne had asked the question, but it was for Quinn and for herself that she told the story.

"For millennia or more, I reveled in my demon-ness, in my powers. I did a lot of bad things. One of them was cursing your family." She paused to drink. "But after a long while, after being with and dealing with humans, I realized I could be different. That I didn't have to accept my fate, didn't have to be like all the rest of my kin. So, I started to find ways to go topside." She watched Quinn as she spoke. She really needed him to understand this.

"I started to possess people and live their lives for as long as I could. I picked people who were looking for a way out. For those who were sick or dying. While I possessed them, they would heal. I tried to give them a second chance at life, even if it was with my soul invading their bodies." She swallowed, hoping Quinn would understand what she was trying to tell him.

His eyes widened. "Rachel? Rachel was dying? That's why you possessed her?"

She set her drink down on the table. "She had ovarian cancer. She would've died in a couple of years. I gave her more than ten."

He jumped to his feet. "Jesus, Daeva. I didn't know."

"I know you didn't."

He rubbed at his face. "I didn't even give you a chance to tell me."

"It's okay, Quinn. It's in the past."

"It's not. I'm such an ass." He fled the living room and went into the guest room.

Leanne tipped her glass. "Looks like the two

of you got a lot of stuff to resolve before the end."

Daeva looked at the Cree woman for a long moment, her throat constricting. "You see much, Leanne Blackbird."

"Yeah, it's another curse I have. Seeing the truth in all things."

Daeva stood, intending to go to Quinn. "And what do you see for Quinn and me?"

Leanne drained her glass and wiped at her mouth. "I think you already know that answer."

Daeva nodded, then walked across the room to the back bedroom. When she went in, Quinn was sitting on the bed, his head in his hands. He looked up at her and she could see the guilt, remorse and pain in his eyes.

A week ago she would've given anything for Quinn to feel this badly for what he'd done to her, but now, now she just wanted to be with him. Time was too short to waste with the past. It was today that mattered.

She sat beside him.

"I'm so sorry, Daeva. I've misjudged you for so long."

"It doesn't matter anymore." She ran her hand through his hair, loving the feel of it against her palm. "The only thing that matters is right now. And us together."

He brought his hand up to her face and cupped her cheek. He rubbed his thumb over her lips.

"I've missed you," he murmured.

Tugging him down to the mattress with her, she wrapped her hand in his hair and covered his mouth with hers, claiming him. At least for now. The kiss was fierce and full of unrequited love and passion. She broke away and looked up at him, wondering if he felt the same way.

As an answer, he fisted her hair, dragging her up to his mouth. He crushed himself to her. She opened her mouth, letting him savage it with his tongue, groaning as he teasingly bit at her bottom lip. This was a different Quinn. An aggressive Quinn. And she liked it.

With one hand still wrapped in her hair, he used the other to grab the front of her T-shirt, ripping it away, leaving her bare breasted. Her nipples hardened in the cool air of the room. He pulled her head back, exposing her neck to his hot, hungry mouth. His hand dipped down to mold her breast with his palm, squeezing her just a little.

Daeva hung on to his shoulders, his arms, anywhere she could gain purchase as he ravished her. She had been taken before, but not with such force, with such need.

Usually reserved and diplomatic, Quinn couldn't be pushed. But in the bedroom, he was the one who liked to push and prod. This was where he took over, where he had always commanded her.

Something animal in her broke, and she clawed at his clothes, desperate to find his flesh, to taste, to feed on every inch of him. She'd been hungry for too long. She ripped open his shirt, her hands finding his smooth skin and hard muscles. Her hands streaked everywhere at once, needing to feel him close, to feel secure.

Dragging his mouth from her lips down her neck to the fullness of her breasts, Quinn flicked one hard nipple with the tip of his tongue. Her skin was soft and smelled of oranges. Saliva pooled in his mouth just at the thought of her. He wanted to feast on her body for a whole night. And even then he wasn't sure he'd be sated.

Restraint broken, he grabbed her around the

waist and tossed her backward on the bed. She gasped in shock but her eyes clouded over with desire. He tore off the remainder of his shirt, shucked his jeans and shorts, then crawled onto the bed.

She let him come, a coy little smile on her lips. His cock hardened at the sight. She was the sexiest woman he'd ever seen. Everything about her pulled at his most primal needs.

He undid her pants, tugged them down her legs, pulled them off and tossed them to the floor. He gripped a leg in each hand, and spreading them, he pulled her forward, sliding her across the mattress until he was nestled tight between her thighs. Her hot, wet center nuzzled his cock and he had to bite down on his lip to stop from burying himself in her. He wanted to take her slowly, to watch every inch of his hard length sink into her silky, warm core.

He looked down at her, so open, so vulnerable, and drank every part of her in. "God, woman, you drive me mad."

"Then do something about it," she teased, as she ran her hands over her breasts.

Gripping his cock in one hand, he guided himself into her. She was so silky wet that he slid in unhindered. He settled a hand on each of her legs and slowly pulled himself out then thrust back in, taking his time, although it killed him to go slow.

Daeva moaned with every thrust. He teased her with his rhythm, moving with slow deliberation at first, then picking up the pace until he was pounding into her mercilessly. With every movement, he could feel her core tightening around him. Squeezing him.

"Harder," she panted.

He fulfilled her wish and buried himself deep inside her. He let go of her legs and fell over her, settling his face into the crook of her neck. She wrapped her legs around his waist and tilted her pelvis up to meet him.

He thrust into her again and again until they both had sweat pouring off their bodies. He gripped her shoulders and pulled her down as he pushed up. He groaned as his body started to quiver with need and desire. One more powerful thrust and he drove hard, emptying himself into her. Raking her nails down his back, she cried out and followed him down the orgasmic spiral into pure bliss.

Chapter 23

The sun was just starting to rise by the time they got on the road the next day. They drove for a couple of hours to the turnoff marked on the map.

Leanne parked the vehicle on a graveled pad. There was a sign that read *Beware of Bears* posted, big and bold, before the metal barrier separating the road from the forest. Nothing like an omen to start a journey, Quinn thought.

Daeva stood beside him as he looked at the sign. "Well, if bears are the only thing we have to deal with, this trip is going to be a piece of cake." She hefted her pack over her shoulder and followed Leanne into the woods.

At first, the trail was easy. It was well-trod and marked, through flat, wooded land. Then they broke out into a clearing and it was evident it was going to get a helluva lot more difficult from there on. There was no clearly marked path, and it was all mountains and valleys for the next ten miles.

Quinn was in shape and healthy, but this was going to kill him, he was sure. He glanced at Daeva and saw the same look on her face.

Leanne on the other hand, looked as if she could hike for another ten hours and not even be winded. She squinted into the high sky. "We'll hike for five hours more, then make camp."

Quinn wasn't going to argue. He was sure in five hours he'd be ready to collapse.

Leanne started the climb up the rise to the next copse of trees. Daeva followed, Quinn beside her.

"How are you faring?" he asked her.

"I'm good," she said, but he could see the sweat dotting her forehead and upper lip.

"Are you sure? You could transfer some of your gear to my pack."

She shook her head. "I can carry my load. I'm fine, Quinn, really."

But he could see she wasn't fine. Ever since the teleportation she'd been weakened. Far more than she was letting on. But he wouldn't press her on the issue. She was stubborn and she would take his concern for her as being vulnerable. He knew she hated feeling that way. So, he would keep his worries to himself, at least for now.

After another two hours of walking, they stopped for water and some sustenance. Daeva dropped her pack and found a fallen tree to sit on. He watched her drink from the canteen and noticed that her T-shirt was soaked with sweat.

He set his pack down next to hers and proceeded to rifle through it, taking out the heavy stuff and setting it down on his pack.

She jumped to her feet. "What are you doing?"

"Helping you."

"I don't need any help." She grabbed at the bedroll he'd taken.

"Yes, you do, Daeva. Don't be…"

"If you call me stupid or dumb I'm going to smack you upside the head."

"I was going to say foolish. I can see how much you are suffering. You're still too weak to be carrying all this."

She stopped making grabs for stuff and just stood by and watched as he loaded his pack with the extra weight. When he was finished, he helped her with her lessened burden.

He kissed her on the forehead, running a hand over her hair. "You're welcome." He caught her half smile before she turned to get back on the trail behind their guide.

They hiked for another three hours, stopping intermittently for water and rest. Daeva was definitely doing better without the extra weight on her back, but she still looked exhausted. As if time itself was taking its toll on her.

Leanne found a small clearing in the trees and declared it the best spot to make camp. There was plenty of tree cover and a narrow stream nearby to provide them with fresh drinking water.

They were all pretty quiet as they pitched tents, one for Leanne and the other for Daeva and Quinn. Once that was done, Leanne went about constructing a fire pit. Daeva announced she was going to fill their canteens at the stream.

Quinn watched her go, a feeling of helplessness filling him. He didn't know how to help her, because he didn't know exactly what was wrong.

"She's dying, you know."

Quinn swirled around to gape at Leanne. "Excuse me?"

"She's been losing her life force since you brought her to me. Every hour a little more disappears."

"Did she tell you that?"

She shook her head. "She didn't have to. I can see it."

"You're wrong. She can't die. She's a demon. They're immortal."

"She is less demon than you think." Leanne stood wiping her hands on her pants. "I know you can see it too, Quinn."

He shook his head, his gut clenching. "I thought she was healing. I was sure of it."

"Ask her. You will know if she's telling you the truth."

After tossing his bedroll into the tent, Quinn went to find Daeva. He found her crouched by the water's edge, splashing her face. She stood when he approached.

"Checking up on me?"

He searched her face, looking for some sign of Leanne's truth. She was pale, definitely, skin slicked with sweat, and her eyes did have a distant look to them. But did that necessarily mean she was dying?

"You're more than drained from the teleportation, aren't you?"

She frowned. "What are you talking about?"

"You said there was a price to pay for the spell. It was your life, wasn't it?"

Her gaze flitted away from him.

"Are you dying, Daeva?"

"What makes you ask that?"

"Can't you just answer the question?"

She was quiet, her eyes settling on everything but him.

He took hold of her arm forcing her to look at him. "Is it because you are bound to me, to the Earth?"

Her gaze lifted to his. She didn't need to answer because he saw the truth in the stormy, gray pools of her eyes. "It doesn't matter, Quinn. All that matters is keeping the chest safe."

He didn't want to believe it. He didn't want to face that truth. There had to be a mistake.

"What if I release you? Would you get your life back?"

Her eyes widened at that. "Why would you even suggest that? It's against everything you stand for. Everything an exorcist is. Your dad was killed by a freed demon."

He gripped her arms tight, pulled her to him. "I would do it for you."

Tears welled in her eyes. And it broke him inside to see them. As they rolled down her cheeks, he wiped them away. "Say something. Please."

"You would risk all that you are for me?"

"Yes."

She fisted her hands in his shirt and leaned into him, pressing her lips to his. She kissed him hard and he responded in kind, burying one hand in the long silky fall of her hair.

They stood on the stream's edge feasting on each other, desperate for each other. Then, spent, Quinn pulled back, resting his forehead against hers. The taste of her was strong on his lips. Forever, he would remember her flavor, strong but sweet like honey.

"I can perform the ceremony right away. I just need my chalk."

She shook her head. "I don't want you to."

He pulled back to search her face. "Why? You'll die if I don't."

"Because once I am released, I will end up back in hell. I won't go back, Quinn, no matter what."

"But if I don't...you'll die."

She shrugged. "I always said I wanted to be fully human. And this is what it is to be human. To face mortality."

He shook his head, angry and frustrated with her attitude. "It's stupid if I can save you."

She gave him a half smile that was infinitely sad. "You have already saved me, Quinn. You did the moment I met you. You made me realize what being human was really about."

He felt weak inside. And guilty. He'd tossed away the best thing that had ever happened to him because of his fear and ignorance.

"I'm sorry."

"For what?"

"For being so stupid three years ago. For not listening to you, for not believing in our love enough."

She kissed him softly, lingering on his lips. "I forgive you."

He sighed. "How long do you think you have?"

She shrugged. "I don't know. I hope it's enough to do what I need to do."

"We'll make it enough. Even if I have to carry you the rest of the way."

More tears ran down her cheeks, and he kissed them away.

Chapter 24

Daeva snuggled into Quinn's warmth inside the sleeping bag. After their moment at the stream, they had returned to camp, eaten, talked with Leanne about the next leg of their trip, then sat and watched the fire, listening to the sounds of the forest. They had sat side by side in comfortable silence. There had been nothing to say, not yet anyway. They'd saved their communication until they were alone in their tent.

And now they were.

Bringing his hand up, he cupped her cheek, bringing her down to his mouth and kissing her.

It was a beautiful, beguiling kiss that plucked at her heart.

Moaning into his mouth, she trailed her hand down his body. She needed to feel him in her hand. He was hot and heavy against her palm, like silk and steel meshed together. She stroked him once, then twice, until he broke the kiss and gasped.

"I want you, Daeva," he groaned. "I have to be inside you now."

"And you will have me," she breathed. "You'll always have me."

Insane with need, she rolled him onto his back and lay on top of him. Purring low in her throat, she pressed kisses to his chin and neck. She trailed her tongue over his pulse points and up to the lobe of his ear to suck it into her mouth. All the while, she continued to stroke him with a fevered pace.

Still gripping his hard length, Daeva pushed aside the cover and moved down his body until she was straddling his thighs. Leaning forward, she flicked her tongue over the tip of his cock. Quinn clamped his eyes shut and moaned as she took him into her mouth. She licked and sucked on him until she could feel his legs quivering. She wanted him like this, vulnerable to her.

"I can't hold on," he panted.

She held him still until he softened a little and retained his control. Then she licked down the length of him, wanting him to lose it all over again. "Yes, you can."

His eyes were dark and hooded. The muscles ticked along the rugged line of his jaw. She loved that look about him. Dark, fierce, barely holding on. She'd remembered that look from their past and would carry it with her for the hours she had left.

After one final stroke of her tongue, she moved up his body to straddle his hips. The delay was destroying her. She'd waited long enough to find bliss. She held him firmly in her hand as she lowered herself. Inch by exquisite inch, he filled her. He was a big man, but still the perfect size for her. When she was fully seated, she held herself still and looked at him. The man she loved. The man who had given her the only thing she'd ever thought she couldn't possess from humanity.

She rubbed her hands up and down his chest, enjoying the way his hard muscles felt under her palms. Watching his face, she contracted the muscles of her sex, squeezing him tight inside her. Every flicker and grimace of emotion that flashed over his handsome face gave her fierce pleasure.

As she started to rock her hips, Quinn reached up and molded her breasts in his hands. He squeezed and flicked his thumbs over her nipples. Waves of pleasure swept over her and she arched her back to catch them cresting. Up and down, back and forth, she moved on him, finding a rhythm, squeezing her muscles with every stroke.

She watched his beautiful face contort with strain as she quickened her pace. She knew he struggled for control and that he was quickly losing it as she took him up and over. There was a sense of power in that, and she reveled in it.

"You're so beautiful, my Daeva," he panted while he moved one hand down to where they joined. He circled his fingers into her slick core, finding her clit with expert ease.

He stroked her as she stroked him. Firmly, pushing her toward climax. Biting down on her lip she tried to stop from screaming out his name. She didn't want to alert Leanne. Although the Cree woman surely knew the sounds of pleasure.

Grabbing hold of his shoulders, she picked up her pace, moving faster, harder, taking them to the edge. As the first crest of orgasm mounted inside, she dug her nails into his flesh. With a loud drawn-out moan, she pushed down on him, filling herself completely with his hot male flesh.

He pressed down on her sensitive bundle of nerves one more time and flipped her over the edge. She collapsed forward onto his chest as she spiraled toward her climax. He wrapped his arms around her, burying himself deep, soaring over into ecstasy with her.

He found her mouth and kissed her hard as the depths of passion drowned them. Everything went white behind her eyes and she thought she'd pass out. But everything was clearer, everything brighter in her mind's eye. And she knew deep down inside that she'd found the true meaning of humanity in this man's arms.

Chapter 25

Daeva heard Leanne outside the tent packing up her gear and getting ready to press on. Careful not to wake Quinn, she slipped out of the sleeping bag and got dressed.

As she crawled out of the tent she saw the sky was just starting to pinken. Her breath came out in plumes as she zipped up her jacket, and she shivered despite the jacket's warmth. She'd been feeling the cold more and more. It was as if a sliver of ice had been imbedded in each of her bones. She couldn't shake it. The warmest she'd been was next to Quinn, basking in his body heat inside the sleeping bag. But she couldn't go back there now.

She found Leanne at the fire, drinking a cup of instant coffee. She offered some to Daeva. "It's not great but it'll warm you."

Daeva took the offered cup and drank the hot liquid. It scalded her tongue and throat on the way down but she didn't care. Anything was better than the blistering cold inside.

Leanne watched her. "It leaves you quickly."

Daeva nodded, knowing exactly what Leanne was talking about. "I don't know how long I have. Twenty-four hours maybe."

"We will be at the mine in four hours. I hope you know where to look once we are there, because the mine has many tunnels, some of them sure to have collapsed. It will be very easy to get lost."

"Once I'm inside, I should be able to feel where the chest is."

They drank in silence for a while, listening to the breeze rustle the leaves. Daeva found it so peaceful, right here, right now. Peace that she'd never thought she'd ever have in her life.

"Does he know?" Leanne asked her.

"He knows enough for it to hurt him."

Leanne nodded, then dumped the last dregs of coffee out of her cup. "We should get going. Time's more important than ever, now."

As Leanne finished packing, Daeva stared at the tent where Quinn still slept. She knew she had to wake him, knew that they needed to move on if they wanted to get to the mine in time, but it was that time she feared. The closer she got to the mine, to the chest, the closer she came to losing everything that mattered to her.

Less than an hour later, they were all packed up and making their way through the trees and past the stream. Quinn hadn't said much since she'd woken him. She wasn't surprised. She didn't have much to say, either. They had expressed themselves last night in the most intimate way. She knew he loved her. There wasn't anything else she really needed to hear.

The final walk wasn't as arduous as before. She had less weight on her back and but also in her heart. Her steps weren't nearly as heavy.

Daeva wondered if this was what it was like to accept one's mortality. She'd always been curious about death and loss. Now she was getting intimately acquainted. It wasn't so bad. Not really. She'd lived a very long life. Seen more, done more than any mortal could even comprehend. But when she glanced at Quinn behind her on the path, she realized that he'd given her more than any and all of her experiences combined. Love had always been the ultimate prize she'd longed for. And he'd given it to her.

Maybe she could die peacefully, knowing she'd experienced the greatest thing worth living for.

They stopped less frequently during the last leg of their journey. They were all anxious to finish. All for different reasons, she suspected. Especially Leanne. Once at the mine, she'd have fulfilled her part of the curse. Daeva just hoped she could lift it as promised. Just because she'd put it on didn't necessarily mean she could easily erase it. Demon magic wasn't so straightforward, even for a demon. There were a lot of hoops to jump through.

As they neared the entrance to the mine, Daeva sensed they were not alone. And it wasn't the bird and critters that had always been there, surrounding them. No, this was something else. Something unnatural. Sorcerer magic had that unnatural tinge to it.

Leanne must've sensed it, as well, because she had the rifle poised and ready to shoot.

Daeva dropped back to Quinn and whispered, "We aren't alone."

His gaze darted to the left then to the right. "The Cabal?"

She nodded. "I think so."

"How did they find us?"

"I didn't set up wards last night. I wasn't thinking straight."

He gripped her shoulder and squeezed. "It's not your fault."

"Regardless, it's too late to worry about it. I say we make a run for it."

"Do you have the energy?"

"I have enough."

"Okay." He broke stride and caught up to Leanne to tell her the plan.

The guide slung her gun around her shoulder then looked to Daeva. Without a word, she sprinted up the rise. Quinn and Daeva were right behind her.

They tore up a small hill. Once on top, Daeva could see the boarded-up entrance to the mine in the valley below. They'd have to cross open land to reach it. There was no other choice.

She dumped her pack—she wouldn't need the meager supplies now—and raced down the hill. This was a one-way trip for her now. As she ran behind Quinn, she glanced quickly to the left side. She saw two sorcerers emerge from the trees about twenty feet away. Two fiery, green balls of magic splattered the ground near her feet. But she kept running.

Quinn looked over his shoulder at her.

"Go!" She waved at him to keep going.

More green fire landed near her, a few sparks landing on her pants. Instantly they burned through the fabric and seared her skin. She patted the fire out with her hand but didn't slow her pace.

The sorcerers were closing in, running just as quickly as she was, maybe more so. It wouldn't be long before they hit her, or worse, hit Quinn or Leanne. As Daeva sprinted the last of the way, her lungs burning, her muscles screaming in agony, she fisted her hands together and concentrated on the fire inside her. Two perfect spheres of red flames formed in her palms.

Turning, she flung them toward their pursuers. One ball hit its mark. Searing fire engulfed the sorcerer's head as he dropped to the ground. The other dodged the assault and kept on coming.

In the meantime, Leanne had reached the mine's entrance and she was kicking at the boards that crisscrossed over it. She wasn't making any headway. When Quinn arrived, he took out the pickax and started to hack at the wood. It wouldn't be fast enough.

Daeva dodged another assault from the remaining sorcerer just as she formed two more balls in her hands. She was barely seven feet from the mine now.

"Out of the way!" she shouted.

Leanne and Quinn both dived for cover as Daeva flung her magic at the mine's entrance. The wood disintegrated into charbroiled splinters that rained down over both of them and the ground.

Nearing the now-open entrance, Daeva grabbed at Quinn to get him up and going. Leanne was already sprinting through the opening. Daeva and Quinn came in, breathing hard, after her. A spray of green followed them in, kicking up dirt and debris.

She looked at Quinn and Leanne. "Are you both okay?"

Leanne nodded.

Quinn took her arm. "You're hurt." He was looking down at the holes in her pants where she could see the red and raw skin of her leg.

"It's nothing." She nudged him away. "We have to get deep inside the mine but we can't have them follow."

"What do you suggest?"

She glanced up at the tunnel roof, held precariously by an old wooden frame. "Cave-in."

"That'll trap us, as well," Leanne said.

Daeva looked at Leanne. "I know."

Another blast of green fire hit the dirt wall beside Quinn. Rocks and wooden slivers pelted him in the side of the face. Blood spotted his cheek where a piece had nicked him.

"I think we're screwed either way." He wiped the blood from his skin.

Daeva nodded. "Move back into the mine. I don't want to crush you."

After flicking on her flashlight, Leanne obeyed. Quinn hung back with Daeva.

"You're expending a lot of energy."

"I know, but it has to be done."

He leaned in and stole a kiss. "Don't kill yourself in the process."

"I won't."

With that, he followed the faint light trail Leanne left with her bouncing flashlight.

Once he was safely away, Daeva concentrated on all the fire inside her. She built it into her hands, creating a huge scarlet wave of power oscillating between her palms. Closing her eyes, she directed everything she had into that moving stream until it was huge and barely containable.

After taking a deep breath, she directed that pulse at the ceiling near the mine's entrance. It had the desired effect. The wooden frame burst apart, and rock and dirt and slate fell to the ground, completely blocking all access to the mine.

There was no way the sorcerers could get in quickly. And no way Daeva, Quinn and Leanne were getting out. At least, not this way.

Once Daeva was certain the entry was sealed tight, she jogged down the dark tunnel in search of the others.

Chapter 26

"Everything go okay?" Quinn asked Daeva as she came alongside him at the Y of two tunnels.

She nodded. "As well as it could. They won't get through."

"Which way?" he asked her.

Leanne shone the light down one, then the other tunnel. Both were cramped and narrow offering no hint as to what lay beyond them. Already the stagnant air was pressing down on his lungs. He couldn't imagine being down here for long, but he suspected that was exactly what was going to happen unless they suddenly stumbled upon the chest then miraculously found another way out.

Daeva pressed her hand to the rock wall on the left. She closed her eyes, and frowned. Then she moved to the other side and did the same. Her frown was a little less this time.

"This way." She pointed toward the right-hand tunnel, then stepped into it, wobbling a bit on her feet. Quinn grabbed her arm to stop her.

"Just wait for a second. Make sure you're okay."

"I'm fine, Quinn."

"You're not. You can barely walk." He pulled her to him, stroking a hand over her hair.

She sighed, leaning into him a little. "I'll be okay. Let's just keep going. When we reach the chest, I'll rest, I promise."

He kept her gaze, gauging whether she was being truthful or not, then pressed a quick kiss to her forehead. "Okay."

Leanne led the way with the only flashlight they'd been able to hold on to. Quinn went next with Daeva behind him, since she was the only one of them able to see in the dark.

They walked for no more than fifteen minutes before the tunnel seemed to get smaller.

Nearer the entrance, the ceiling barely brushed the top of his head, but now he found he had to tilt his head sideways to avoid knocking it against the wooden beams holding up the tons of rock and dirt overhead.

"Is this getting smaller or am I hallucinating?"

"No, it's getting smaller," Leanne said. "Gets even worse up ahead. I think we might have to crawl through."

Leanne was correct in her assumption. Another three feet and the ceiling dropped considerably. It looked as though there had been a partial cave-in a long time ago. Just what Quinn needed to think about while he was feeling claustrophobic.

"I guess we crawl," Daeva said, as she dropped to her hands and knees. "I'll go first, just in case."

"In case of what?" Quinn asked.

"In case it falls again." Without waiting for his response, she started on.

He knew arguing with her was pointless, so he followed her instead. Leanne brought up the rear.

They crawled over stone and dirt for the next

twenty minutes. Every once in a while, Quinn would look up, envisioning the ceiling collapsing on him. He had to stop once and remember how to breathe because he was having difficulty doing just that.

"Not much farther," Daeva said, but he was sure she'd said it only to reassure him.

But, true to her word, after another five minutes of crawling and scraping through rock and wood debris, the tunnel opened up into a cavern. Daeva formed a glowing ball of demon light and set it loose. It drifted up in the cavern casting an eerie glimmering over the rock.

Quinn pushed to his feet and, lifting his head, took in several deep breaths. The air was hot and heavy in the cavern, but at least it was plentiful.

Happy to be in one piece, Quinn swung around to share it with Daeva. His joy dissipated. He found Daeva still on her hands and knees, rocking back and forth, her eyes closed.

He rushed to her side and helped her to sit up against one of the rock walls. Her skin was so cold, he thought she was dead. He touched her cheek, then ran his fingers down to her neck to check her pulse. He found it, but it was faint. Her breath came in short shallow pants.

Leanne crouched beside them, taking up Daeva's wrist and holding her fingers over the pulse point. "Her heart pumps, but it is slow."

"What can we do?" he asked, but he knew there was nothing. Nothing that Daeva would allow him to do.

Leanne patted his shoulder. "Pray."

"Please, don't," Daeva groaned.

Relief surged through him. "I thought maybe you decided to leave me." He brushed her damp hair from her brow.

"Nah, you can't get rid of me that easily."

"I don't want to ever get rid of you."

Her eyes opened, and she reached up and touched his cheek. "I know."

"I'm going to get you out of here."

She shook her head. "Have to find the chest first."

"Screw the chest, let the world handle its own shit."

She gave him a small smile. "You don't really mean that."

"Yeah, I do."

"Well, you don't have to go far, because the

chest is here." She lifted her hand and pointed high on the rock wall.

"In the wall?"

She nodded. "Going to need to dig it out."

Leanne stood, went over to her pack, and unstrapped a pickax. She walked to the wall, hefted it, and swung at the rock with a thunk. Little pieces of rock scattered on the stone ground.

Quinn watched her swing again. It was going to take more than that to find the chest. It would take both of them digging at the rock. But he didn't have an ax. They'd only brought the one.

"How deep is it?" he asked Daeva.

"Deep enough."

After he made sure Daeva wasn't going to collapse sideways, Quinn went over to Leanne and took the pickax from her. He hefted it over his head and started to dig.

Working at the rock wall took its toll on Quinn. Sweat slicked his face and back. His T-shirt stuck to him like glue. The muscles in his arms quivered with strain with every swing of the ax. And he hadn't gotten all that far. There was maybe a three-foot-deep hole at best. But no chest.

He took a break and sat beside Daeva as Leanne took up the chore of hacking at the rock wall. He drank from the canteen, then offered some to Daeva. She shook her head, refusing the water.

"You need it."

"You need it more. Don't waste it on me."

Quinn's heart squeezed. He hated to hear the defeat in her voice. It was like a spear to his soul.

"Don't give up, Daeva. I won't let you give up."

She blinked up at him, the whites of her eyes bloodshot, a sheen of sweat on her forehead. "You're going to have to let me go, Quinn."

"No, I don't." He cupped her cheek. "I did that once before, and I won't do it again."

"It's okay, you know. I understand why you did what you did. I should've told you from the beginning. I should never have kept such a secret from you."

"If you had we might not have had the years we had together."

She nodded, then smiled. "True."

"I wouldn't give up those years for anything,

I'm glad we had them. I'm glad we had this time together."

"Me, too."

He leaned over and brushed his lips against hers. "I love you."

"I love you, too."

Then there came an audible bang, followed by Leanne's awe-filled voice.

"I found it."

Chapter 27

"Help me up," Daeva demanded, her lungs burning with the effort of breathing.

Quinn hauled her to her feet. Leaning heavily on him, she moved toward the hole in the rock wall where Leanne stood staring. Daeva looked into the stone and saw the corner of a wooden box.

"That's the chest."

"It looks lodged in there pretty good," Quinn said. "How the hell are we going to get it out without breaking it? We don't want to damage the book."

Daeva shuffled closer to the wall. "I can melt it out."

Quinn held her back. "You'll waste your energy. You need it to…"

"To what? This is a one-way trip for me, Quinn. You're the one that will need to get it out of here and protect it."

She saw in his eyes that he wanted to argue with her. But he remained silent. Maybe because he knew she'd do what she willed. And the fact that she was right. She was near her end. There was no getting out of here for her.

Nodding, he let her go.

She stepped up to the wall, and set her hands on the rock surrounding the edge of the chest. Closing her eyes, she searched for the last dregs of demon fire inside. There wasn't much there. Enough, she hoped, to melt the stone and not set the wood on fire.

She gathered it in and forced it through her arms to her hands. Her palms began to warm. The energy grew gradually until there was a heat that burned her skin. Normally, that wouldn't have happened, but she was mortal now. Things were different for her.

It took longer than usual to heat the rock. She

pushed the fire through her hands with all her strength. Soon, she could feel the stone give. It grew pliable and liquid. Opening her eyes, she watched as it dripped, bit by bit, down the wall, unearthing even more of the chest until the entire three-cubic-foot box was visible.

Bone weary, she took a step back so Quinn and Leanne could get in there and pry the chest loose using what tools they had. She stumbled, then managed to settle herself down to the floor as they wrangled it out of its century-long stone imprisonment. They set it down beside her.

Daeva set her hand on top of the elaborately inscribed wooden chest, feeling the power inside vibrating against her palm. "It's bigger than I remember."

"It's heavy," Leanne commented. "I'm not sure how we're going to carry it out."

"You won't have to." Daeva grabbed the chest to turn it around. Quinn was there to help. Once it was turned, she ran her fingers over the elaborate lock.

"The Cabal have the key," Quinn said.

"No, they don't." She lifted her arm. "Someone give me a knife."

Leanne unsheathed the small blade on her hip and handed it to Daeva.

She took it and slid it along her arm where a three-inch scar marked her skin. Pain shot up her arm but she kept at it until rivulets of blood rolled off the tips of her fingers to dot the rocky ground beside her.

"What the hell are you doing?"

"Remember Loir? The little goblin that beat you up at your house?"

Quinn nodded. "Very well."

Daeva smiled. "She's very loyal to me." She set the knife down next to her. "She switched the key with a fake and gave me the real one."

"Okay, so why are you slicing up your arm?"

"Because I needed a place to hide it." Biting down on her lip, she split her skin with her fingers and dug into her flesh. More agony made her head swim but she persevered until finally she pulled out the key.

Quinn looked queasy as he plucked the gore-covered key from her hand. "Unbelievable. Why didn't you tell me?"

"A girl likes to keep a little mystery once in a while."

He shook his head, trying hard not to look at

the blood still running down her arm. "You have more than a little mystery, Daeva, trust me."

"Well, are you going to use it or not?" She gestured to the chest.

After wiping the key on his shirt, Quinn crouched next to her and slid the key into the lock. She could see his hands shaking. He turned it, and there was an audible click and then a puff of air as the lid released. Slowly, he opened it.

Inside was a book. It was the grimoire that King Solomon used to summon the demons to do his work. It should've looked ominous or important, but it didn't. It looked like a plain black leather-bound book with yellowing pages.

Quinn lifted it out, turned it over and looked at her. "This is it?"

She nodded. "Looks normal, doesn't it?"

"Yes. It's strange."

"Here, let's put it in your pack."

She reached over and grabbed Quinn's backpack, dragging it toward her. She unzipped it and took out one of Quinn's T-shirts, then took the book and wrapped it in the innocuous material. She shoved it into his pack.

"There. Done." She handed the pack to Quinn, avoiding his gaze.

"Daeva, I'm not leaving without you."

She looked at the ground, the threat of tears stinging her eyes. "Don't be an idiot, Quinn. You have to go."

"I'll carry you out of here."

She shook her head. "Don't waste your time. I'm already dead."

He gripped her chin in his fingers and forced her to look at him. "I will not leave you. Ever."

She stared into his eyes and saw the truth there. The realization that he wouldn't leave her, even when she asked him to. And wasn't that one of the reasons she loved his stubborn ass so much?

"Fine. Get me up, then."

He helped her to her feet. Her head swam and her vision wavered but she kept on her feet. She leaned on him, but felt maybe she could walk.

She gestured to the tunnel to the left. "If we follow that one, we should find another way out."

Quinn nodded, but Leanne didn't look convinced. "Are you sure?"

"No, but it's better than sitting here and waiting for the air supply to run out."

Without another word, Leanne held up the flashlight and walked toward the tunnel.

Quinn put an arm around Daeva. "I'll carry you if you can't walk."

"I can walk." And to prove her point she took a baby step forward, then another. "See?"

Unsatisfied, he started toward the tunnel, helping her with every step.

Fortunately, this tunnel was wider than the last one. Crawling through that had been hard. Daeva had been in a lot of tight spaces before—being in hell prepares a demon for a life of small, cramped spaces with no breathable air—but that one had filled her with terror. This mortality thing was surprising in so many awful ways.

They'd traveled for maybe a half hour when Daeva heard something that made her stomach roil and her heart leap into her throat.

"Do you hear that?" she whispered.

Leanne stopped in front of them and turned around. "I don't hear anything."

"What do you hear?" Quinn asked.

"Water."

As soon as she said the word, a trickle of water washed forward from behind them. She looked down at her feet as the swell covered her boots.

Quinn's eyes widened. "They're flooding us."

"We need to go right now."

"I'm going to carry you." He reached down to hook her legs. But Daeva nudged him back.

"I can run."

"Daeva…"

"Go. I will follow. I promise."

Leanne led the charge. After a lingering look, Quinn turned and followed her, his boots slapping in the slowly rising water.

Daeva watched his retreating back and wondered where she was going to find the reserves to follow. Leaning against the tunnel wall, she watched as the water level reached her ankles. It wouldn't be long before it reached her knees, then her waist. If she couldn't walk now, she'd never be able to move through the weight of the water.

Closing her eyes, she took in a deep breath then let it out slowly. It was now or never.

She opened her eyes and took a step forward, then another, then another, until she was running through the pools, water splashing up onto her pants legs. Soon, she was right behind Quinn. He glanced over his shoulder and she saw the relief in his eyes.

The sound of rushing water echoed through the shaft as they ran. Daeva could see the trickles down the rock faces on either side. Water sloshed around her knees. It was getting harder to run. She was already using the last of her energy reserves. It wouldn't be long before her legs gave out. And when she fell, she knew she'd never get up again.

"I see a light up ahead," Leanne called back to them.

"Run toward it," Daeva responded, even as she slowed. The water was up to her thighs now.

Quinn stopped and grabbed her hand, tugging her forward. "Hang on to me."

She shook her head. "I'll hold you back."

"Don't let go, Daeva."

She nodded to him as he pulled her forward. As they ran together, she concentrated on the feel of Quinn's hand in her own. The warmth of his skin against hers gave her the momentum to power on.

The light up ahead that Leanne had spotted

grew larger. Daeva could see it now. She hoped it was an opening, a way out. If it wasn't, they would all die down in the mine. Definitely not the way she thought she'd die. Well, she never thought she'd die to begin with so she supposed it didn't matter.

Water rose to their waists, and it was becoming harder to move forward. There was a current coming from somewhere pushing them backward. Daeva suspected the current was sorcerer generated.

"There's a hole," Leanne said. "I can see it." There was hope in Leanne's voice.

Daeva nearly shared it. Until she saw the wooden beams on the right side of the tunnel start to give. The cracking sound was deafening.

"Leanne!" she screamed.

Just as Leanne turned to Daeva's voice, the beams broke. An overhead rafter fell, a ton of rock and dirt giving it deadly momentum. The edge hit Leanne across her shoulders and back. She went down, face-first into the water.

Quinn let Daeva's hand go as he reached down to aid Leanne. He lifted her out of the water so she wouldn't drown, but the way her body twisted unnaturally made Daeva's gut roll over. The woman's back had to be broken. She cried out as Quinn tried to get a better grip on her.

"Oh, Jesus, Leanne." He looked at Daeva. "Her back…"

She nodded. "We have to get her out of here." She moved past him as he cradled Leanne to his chest, pushing against the water level to survey the light source.

There was a hole in the rock about eight feet up. She wasn't sure if it was big enough for them to squeeze through, but she'd make it big enough even if it took the last of her life force.

She pointed up toward the opening. "I'm not sure if I can make it bigger."

Carefully floating Leanne on her back, Quinn moved to stand beside Daeva. "Can you reach it?"

She shook her head. "We'll have to wait until the water level rises." It was now at their chests. They'd have to wait until they couldn't touch the ground any longer and it would lift them up.

It didn't take long for the water to reach their necks, it hovered just at Daeva's chin. It was cold and her body started to shiver, taking up valuable vitality. Slowly, the level crept up her face, over her lips to her nose. She pushed up with her toes to tread water.

"Here we go," Quinn said as he, too, started to kick with his legs to keep buoyant.

As they trod water, rising closer to the hole, Leanne floating next to them, Daeva moved closer to Quinn. Not wanting to lose him. Ever.

But she would, no matter what happened.

"Kiss me," she murmured.

He ran a hand over her head, anchoring her there so he could press his lips to hers. The kiss was soft and gentle and full of all the things they wanted to say to each other but didn't have the strength or time to utter.

"We're going to make it out."

"When did you become an optimist?"

He smiled. "The moment I met you."

The tears came then. As they rolled down her cheeks they mingled with the icy water that was still rising.

Looking upward, Daeva lifted her hands and touched the hole. It wasn't even a foot wide. Not big enough for a full body to squeeze through. She gripped the sides and started to dig and pull at the dirt and rock while Quinn held Leanne. Bits and pieces fell into the water around her, but it still wasn't enough. Soon the water level would rise higher than the hole and they would lose room to breathe. They might be able to stick their faces out the hole for air, but how long would that last?

She settled her hands along the sides and forced the tiny sparks inside her to rise to the surface. They came quickly but they were not strong. She fed the fire into the rock. Gritting her teeth, she pushed it harder and harder. A tooth cracked in her mouth and blood started to pool in her throat. She swallowed it and continued to manipulate the demon magic inside her.

She gave it one final push and, finally, the hole gave. Substantial pieces fell on top of her head and rolled into the frigid waters.

"Get her out," she said to Quinn.

He floated to the wide hole and pulled himself up, wiggling his body until he was completely out. He reached down to Leanne. Daeva lifted her up to him, trying to be careful of Leanne's injuries but knowing that if they didn't force her through she would die.

With one final tug, he was able to pull her body out. Then he reached down for Daeva.

"Your turn, baby."

She let him grip her arms and she kicked when he pulled. She managed to squirm through with Quinn's help. When she was out, she rolled onto her back and took in deep cleansing breaths of the fresh cool air. Water bubbled out of the hole next to her. A few more minutes under and they would've all drowned.

But now they were safe.

"Well, look what the mine puked out."

Or not.

Daeva blinked up into the sun, and into the shadow of a sorcerer.

Chapter 28

Quinn tried to get to his feet but the boot in his gut forced him down again. He rolled onto his side and looked up into the face of Richter Collins.

"We meet again, Quinn. How fortuitous. For me."

"How's the leg? Still limping?"

Richter smiled but there was no humor or warmth there. His expression was cold and calculating. "Where's the chest?"

"Back in the hole you just filled up."

A muscle in his jaw ticked. Quinn could easily tell that the sorcerer was pissed off that his plan had backfired.

"Well, I guess one of you is going back in to retrieve it."

Richter nudged Leanne with the toe of his shoe. Her head lolled back and forth.

"Don't touch her. She's badly injured."

"I noticed." Then his gaze narrowed on Daeva, who was also lying on her back, arms splayed out, her face pale, her chest barely rising and falling. "Then the demon bitch. She can do it." He reached down to grab her by the hair.

Quinn was up and on him in seconds. "Get off her!"

But he was still so winded and exhausted from the journey that Richter easily backhanded him, sending him sprawling back to the ground. It helped that the sorcerer had magic to back him. Quinn could feel the telltale burn of it across his face.

"Do yourself a favor, exorcist, and stay down."

Another sorcerer stood over Quinn, his hands glowing green, ready to launch an attack at Richter's command.

Richter finished reaching for Daeva and

yanked on her hair to pull her up. She was like a rag doll in his hand.

Fury rolled through Quinn but he couldn't see a way to get to the sorcerer without being fried by the fiery magic balls of doom. Then he saw the miraculous glint of steel at Leanne's hip. He just had to get over there.

Richter dragged Daeva across the dirt by her hair. "What's the matter with your demon, Quinn? Is she broken?"

"She's injured, you dick."

Richter frowned down at her, then waggled her head back and forth. "How can she be injured? Demons can regenerate."

Quinn didn't want to tell the sorcerer that he'd made her mortal by binding her to him and the Earth. It was best that Richter still thought she was a demon. But what if he did something to her that couldn't be taken back?

Richter dropped her by the hole in the ground that they'd just come out of. Water had stopped gushing from it. The ground around it was muddy and slick.

"The water level is going down. So she can go back and get me that chest." He nudged her toward the hole.

It took everything Quinn had not to bolt across the ground, wrap his hands around Richter's throat and squeeze the life out of him. But he had to time it right—he was going to get one chance to kill this guy and he wasn't going to blow it.

As if privy to his thoughts, Daeva opened her eyes and looked at him. Her lips twitched up into a sad smile. Was she telling him something? He kept watching her, then she mouthed the word...*now*.

She reached up and grabbed Richter's wrists with her hands. Her dark magic absorbed his hands and diminished his own green, glowing sparks.

His eyes widened and he cried out.

Quinn kicked the sorcerer looming over him between the legs and knocked him unconscious with a right hook to the jaw. He then rolled twice to Leanne, and unsheathed her knife. He was on his feet in seconds and moving towards Richter.

The sorcerer pulled Daeva up and slammed her back down to the ground. She relinquished her hold on him, but it was too little too late. Quinn was already on him.

With all the power he could muster, Quinn

jammed the knife into the sorcerer's throat. Surprise widened his eyes and his hands came up to his neck. But it was pointless. There was no way he could stem the flow of blood.

"Told you, asshole, that I'd ram it into your throat next time I saw you."

Gurgling nonsensically, Richter dropped to the ground, blood gushing from his wound and soaking the dirt beneath him. Ignoring him, Quinn rushed to Daeva's side, cradling her to his chest.

"You're okay. Everything's going to be okay." He rocked her back and forth.

She blinked up at him. "Liar." She coughed, her whole body convulsing with the sheer power of it.

He smoothed a hand over her hair, trying hard not to let tears flow. He vowed he wouldn't cry. But the emotion inside him was bubbling up too hard and too fast.

"Stay still, now."

She lifted her hand and touched his cheek. "You're sweet." Then her hand fell to the side. She turned her head to look at Leanne. "How is she?"

Quinn glanced at the Cree woman. "Not

good. I don't think she's going to make it. I don't know how to get her out of here without killing her."

"Move me closer to her."

He frowned. "Why?"

"Because maybe I can do one last thing in this life that's good."

He didn't argue with her. Lifting Daeva gently, he pulled her over to Leanne and settled her down again. Daeva reached over and grabbed Leanne's hand.

"If she wakes, will you tell her I'm sorry about everything?"

He nodded. "Yes, I'll tell her."

"Good." She smiled at him. "Will you always remember me?"

The tears came then. He let them fall, too distraught to wipe them away. "Always and forever."

"I wish we could've had more time together. We had some good times didn't we?"

"The best."

"Liar," she murmured. "Kiss me one last time, Quinn Strom. Let me go into the abyss with the taste of you on my lips."

He leaned down to her mouth and gently

brushed his lips against hers. They kissed, and it was slow and gentle and full of everything they'd yet to experience together. Full of regret for a life they'd never have.

He broke away and looked down at her, brushing his hand over her clammy face. Her skin was like ice now. Her lips were turning blue. It was difficult to watch but he couldn't turn away. He wouldn't let her go without some comfort.

"Thank you."

"You're welcome." He kissed her forehead one last time.

She closed her eyes and gripped Leanne's hand tight. He watched as her chest rose and fell with shallow breaths. He watched and waited, until the last deep breath she took didn't come out. Her face went slack and her fingers uncurled from Leanne's.

Trying hard not to sob, he lifted her body and cradled her against his chest. He nuzzled his face into her hair and breathed in deep. Her smell was still the same. The feel of her in his arms, so right, so perfect.

But gone. Forever.

As he held her tight, rocking back and forth,

he sensed movement beside him. He looked over at Leanne as she opened her eyes.

"Quinn?"

"Are you all right?" he asked, unbelieving.

"I think so." She moved her arms. "What happened?"

"Daeva gave you the last of her life to save you."

Slowly, Leanne sat up and looked at Daeva in his arms. She reached over and touched her cheek. "I saw her in my dream. She kissed me, then I felt warm."

He nodded, more tears rolling down his cheeks. The love of his life was dead. He didn't know how to go on without her.

Leanne put a hand on his shoulder. "You will see her again, Quinn."

"When?" he blubbered. "When I die?"

She shook her head. "I don't know when, but do not give up on her."

He pressed his lips to Daeva's cheek, inhaling her in, needing her to *be*. But knowing she'd never *be* again.

Chapter 29

The darkness was heavy and cloying. It clung to her like too-thick cobwebs. She tried to shake the feeling loose, but it failed. In fact, she wasn't certain she could even move. She tried to shrug her shoulders, but didn't get a sense of any movement. Maybe she didn't have a body anymore.

Am I dead?

Daeva pondered that. Is this what death was? A vast stretch of nothingness?

She really hoped not, as it was going to get pretty boring in the afterlife if all she had to look forward to was absolute darkness. It's not that she expected pearly gates and harps, considering her species, but this nothingness was really quite the disappointment.

To her relief, the darkness eventually faded and she was floating in a sea of twinkly lights. She looked down and saw her form, weightless. She lifted her arm, inspecting her skin. The scar was gone. Her skin was flawless. But she still couldn't *feel* her arm moving.

She grabbed one of the twinkly lights with her hand. She held it there until it warmed her skin. She opened her hand and watched as the light danced on her palm, changing color from white to green to black. Then it exploded and a thousand shards of black glass shot through the colorless sky around her.

She tracked one of the shards through the air as it zoomed away. It seemed to be following someone. She swore she could see a dark form shimmering on the horizon.

Flapping her arms, she tried to move through the emptiness. It seemed to be working because the dark form in the distance was getting larger and more defined.

The closer she got, the clearer the form became. Daeva could see the long, silky, black hair of the Cree woman whose family she'd cursed.

Leanne? Are you dead, too?

She turned and smiled at Daeva. She shook her head, then held out her hand. Daeva took it, feeling the woman's skin vividly against her own.

Come with me.

Where are we going?

You will see.

Smiling, Daeva let Leanne guide her away from the twinkly lights and down to a bridge. Her feet touched down and she could almost feel the structure under her soles.

Holding hands, the two women strolled down the bridge toward a bright white light.

Will I see Quinn again?

Leanne smiled and nodded. *Yes. In time. But not yet. He has to learn to release you first.*

Although Daeva was sad she wouldn't see Quinn soon, she still felt a lightness inside she'd never experienced before. It was nice and un-expected.

Leanne led her forward, pulling on her hand. At first they were in stride, but eventually Leanne pulled ahead. She yanked on Daeva's hand.

Finally, they were going so fast, everything became a blur. It was as if they were traveling through the ether. Like teleportation. But that wasn't possible, was it?

It went faster and faster, until Daeva couldn't even see herself. Everything was one big white blur. She opened her mouth to scream, to tell Leanne to stop.

And then it did.

Daeva blinked open her eyes.

Chapter 30

The house hadn't been nearly as bad as Quinn thought it was going to be when he returned. Ivy'd had something to do with that, he was sure. He'd called her when they'd been on the road and she promised to take of it. And she had.

There was no police tape, and the living room had been tidied a bit, as had been his bedroom. Minus the hole in the wall. He'd have to take care of that himself. When he got around to it. Right now he didn't feel like doing much of anything.

He stood in the basement and stared at the pentagram still chalked in white on the floor. He'd been staring at it for the past twenty minutes. But he couldn't leave, he couldn't move. Maybe if he looked at it hard enough or long enough, she would magically appear.

He twisted the chalk in his fingers and considered doing another summons. Maybe she was just waiting for him to call her home. Maybe she'd been wrong about dying. Surely a demon could never die. Not even one that was bound to the Earth.

He nudged the open book on the cement floor. It was one of his summoning books. He'd poured over it for the past hour looking for something, anything, that would tell him that she didn't really die. Even a grain of hope would have been enough. But he couldn't find anything.

His last bit of hope had faded when he'd turned the last page.

He shoved the chalk back into his pocket and took out his cell phone. He scrolled through his contacts and dialed a number. Quianna answered on the fourth ring.

"Hey, Quinn."

"I have it, Q."

An hour later he parked in the university visitor's lot and made his way to the faculty building. The backpack weighed heavy on his shoulders. All that was inside was the book, but it was heavier than anything he'd ever carried before. It had cost him so much.

He knocked on her door, waiting for her to tell him to come in. When she did, he went inside and stood by the leather visitor chair. She sat behind her desk, glasses perched on her perky nose.

"So, do you have it?"

Quinn nodded and reached into his backpack, pulling out the fabric-wrapped package. He handed it to her.

She took it gingerly and set it on the desk. Hands shaking, Quianna unfolded the shirt. Inside was the book. "The grimoire that King Solomon used to summon his demons."

She traced a finger over the old black leather. "Amazing. I can feel the power radiating from it." She looked up at him. "I can't believe you found it."

"It wasn't me who found it." He kept his shoulders straight although he wanted to sag forward. The weight of losing Daeva pressed heavily on his mind, body and soul. He wasn't sure he'd ever recover from her loss.

Quianna sat back in her chair, taking off her glasses. "Who was it then?"

"A friend."

"By the look in your face, I'd say more than a friend."

He nodded. "Yeah, she was."

"I'm sorry, Quinn."

"So am I." He got to his feet, swinging the pack over his shoulder. "Well, I'll see you."

"Where are you going?"

"Home."

She nodded. "Thank you for bringing it to me. I'll take care of it now. You go rest. You deserve a break."

He turned and walked out of her office, shutting the door firmly behind him.

With that behind him, maybe now he could move on with his life. The pain in his chest told him it would be an uphill battle all the way. He was one for challenges, but just getting out of bed this morning had been a struggle.

His cell phone thumped from his pants pocket. He fished it out. "Strom."

It was an old friend and hunting partner, Jake. "I have a job for you."

"I'm taking a break from that for a while."

"I think you'll want this one."

Quinn paused, rubbing at the stubble on his chin. Did he really want another job? Is this what he really needed to forget Daeva? "I'm listening."

"I got a lead on Todd Sheppard. Haven't you been looking for him for a few years?"

"What's the address?"

"I'll text it to you."

"Great."

"Do you want some extra help on this? Gi and I could be backup."

"No, thanks, Jake, but I got this. I need this."

"I understand. Take care, buddy."

"You, too." Quinn ended the call, then waited for the text with the address.

This was closure, in a way. Going full circle to the beginning of it all. It would be good for him to end it. Maybe that would help him move on. Or maybe it would just help him deal with the anger still churning inside him.

It didn't surprise Quinn that Todd was hanging out in a nightclub. It was the sorcerer's usual

MO. The guy had no imagination—he was as predictable as they came.

Because of that, it didn't take Quinn long to track him down inside the club. The sorcerer was sitting with a group of women. Quinn searched the table for red hair. For one second his heart thudded expectantly, then it faded when he saw only blondes sitting in the group. Instead of coming at the sorcerer from behind, Quinn decided to approach the subject head on.

He walked up to the table, grabbed an empty chair and sat in it, facing Todd. The sorcerer was about to jump to his feet, but Quinn grabbed his arm and held him in place.

"I'm had the worst week of my life, Todd, you really don't want to piss me off."

The sorcerer must've seen something in Quinn's eyes, because he stayed in his chair. "What do you want?"

"I want you to stop summoning demons to do your dirty work."

At the word demon, the entire group of ladies at the table got up and left.

"I don't know what you're talking about," the sorcerer sniveled.

Quinn slapped him across the face, hard.

"Don't be an idiot, Todd. Confession is good for the soul. You do worry about your soul, don't you?"

Todd swallowed. "I'm leaving the Cabal. I'm not practicing anymore."

"Somehow, I don't believe you."

"It's true. Ever since Richter...you know?" Todd eyed Quinn warily. Obviously he'd heard of the Cabal leader's demise and at whose hand. "I don't want to be involved anymore. It's getting too dangerous."

"You've hurt a lot of people, Todd. You can't walk away from that."

He hung his head. "I know. I'm willing to pay for that."

"Okay."

His head came up, surprise furrowing his brow. "Okay? You're going to let me go?"

"No, I'm going to drop you off at the police station and you're going to confess to hurting those women. And you're going to go to jail and do your time."

"And if I don't?"

"Then I'm going to kill you, Todd. Right here, right now."

Todd looked around, maybe questioning

whether he could get away or not, then he looked back at Quinn. He rubbed a hand over his mouth and leaned back in the chair, sighing. "Fine."

Quinn stood, and pulled Todd to his feet. He escorted the sorcerer out to his car, opened the door and shoved him into the passenger side.

On the way to the police station, Quinn watched Todd out of the corner of eye. "Let me ask you something."

"Okay."

"You've done a lot of demon summoning. Have you ever bound one to the Earth and to yourself?"

Todd nodded. "Once."

"What happened to the demon? Did you send it back?"

Todd looked at him. "No. I was in love. I wanted to be with her forever."

Quinn nodded for him to continue.

"She passed through to the other side, then I released her."

Quinn nearly swerved the car. "What do you mean she passed? She died, right?"

"In a way. They don't die and go back to hell, but sort of stay in a limbo."

"She came back to you? You saw her again?"

The sorcerer nodded, a small smile on his face. "Oh, yeah, after I did the releasing ceremony she came back, all right."

Quinn's heart was racing. He could still find Daeva. There was the hope he was searching for. She wasn't lost to him forever.

Todd turned his head to show Quinn the scar along his neck. "Yup, she came back, nearly ripped my throat out and took off. I haven't seen her since. Some demons are just not meant to be released, I guess."

Quinn pulled up to the curb in front of the station. "We're here. Go do the right thing."

Todd nodded. "Thanks for the reprieve, I guess." He opened the door and slid out. He hesitated on the sidewalk for a moment, then trudged up the steps to the front doors.

Quinn pulled away from the station; Todd was on his own. Quinn had more important things to do. He had the woman he loved to save.

Chapter 31

The second he reached his house, Quinn bolted through the front door and ran down the steps to the basement, nearly tripping on the way.

He grabbed the book on the floor and flipped through it. There had to be a release ceremony in there somewhere. After several minutes of flipping pages and checking the index, he found the ritual he was looking for. It had been there the whole time and he hadn't seen it. Or maybe he hadn't been looking for it.

But he found it, and that was all that mattered right now.

After reading the ritual repeatedly, he set the book down. Grabbing his broom he swept away the initial pentagram. He had to construct a new one, with different symbols in the corners.

On his hands and knees, he drew a pentagram with his blessed chalk. He put the appropriate symbols in the corners. The usual two for a regular summoning, then one for portal, one for travel, and the last for freedom. When he was finished, he stood, took out his blessed blade and slid it across his palm. He squeezed his hand into a fist. Blood dribbled down his wrist. He held his fist over each of the symbols and spoke the words.

"I call you, Daeva, Seductress of the Shadows. I call you to me. I call you to this realm. I call you forth." He waited a few seconds, then closing his eyes, he breathed a sigh. "I call you so I can release you. I call you because I love you."

He waited and watched the pentagram, expecting any moment for the wild red-haired woman to burst into existence. He listened for the telltale popping noise, lifted his nose for the hint of cinnamon that she always carried with her on her skin.

Seconds went by, then minutes. After thirty minutes, Quinn sat down on the cement floor, crossing his legs for comfort. He sat like that, head in hand, staring at the pentagram for another hour.

It didn't work. She wasn't coming back.

He stood, went up the stairs, flicked off the light and slammed the door shut. He walked into the kitchen, opened the cupboard and took out the three-quarters-full bottle of Scotch. Hooking the bottle between his fingers, he went into the living room and sat on the sofa.

Unscrewing the top, he took a long pull. He forewent a glass because the fact of the matter was he didn't plan on regulating his drinking. He planned on getting drunk. So drunk that he would be numb.

His heart and soul throbbed in agony. He never wanted to feel this much pain again. And if he could anesthetize himself, even for a little while, it would be enough. He just couldn't handle it right now. It was too much. Too real. Too intense.

He took another long drink. Soon, though, he wouldn't be feeling a thing.

* * *

Something woke Quinn. A noise. From downstairs.

He rolled over on his bed and put his feet on the floor. He rubbed at his eyes and mouth. He smacked his lips. He had the worst taste in his mouth. After drinking the entire bottle of Scotch, he'd crawled up the stairs, puked in the bathroom and then crawled into the bedroom.

He didn't even know what time it was. It was still dark. He glanced at his watch. Three in the morning. The witching hour.

Thud.

There it was again. Quinn reached under his pillow and slid out his knife. If it was the Cabal again, he wasn't going to be nice this time.

He stood, wobbled once, nearly fell, but righted himself. It was possible he was still a bit drunk.

Gripping his blade defensively, he made it to the door and opened it. He paused in the door frame listening for any more sounds and heard a clinking. Sounded like glass.

He padded to the stairwell, stared down it, looking for any movement. Nothing came. He started down the stairs as silently as possible. At the bottom, he looked toward the living room.

There was no movement or sound from there. He turned toward the kitchen. A shadow moved on the floor.

He slid against the wall, keeping his back tight to the kitchen. Quickly, he peered around the corner. Someone was definitely in there. The refrigerator was hanging open.

Keeping low, he crept into the kitchen, his knife hand out. There was someone there, in front of him, doing something on one of the counters. In the dark, he could see the outline of a person. A person his height, with a very curvy figure…

"Daeva?"

The shape turned, and in the beam of moonlight that cascaded through the kitchen window he could see her face. Her beautiful pale face.

He dropped his knife. "Daeva?"

She smiled around the chicken leg she'd been tearing into. "Hey, baby. I'm sorry I was just so hungry."

He crossed the room in two strides and had her in his arms. The chicken leg dropped as she wrapped her hands in his hair, and held on for dear life while he claimed her mouth with his.

He kissed her hard, like a drowning man in desperate need of oxygen. She tasted of everything he remembered, everything he ever wanted or needed in life.

He broke away from her lips and, cupping her cheeks with his hands, just looked at her. Making sure she was real and not a figment of his inebriated imagination.

"Are you real?" he asked, his voice strained with emotion.

She nodded and smiled. "You bet I am. I'm as real as I'm ever going to get. And that's saying something."

"My summoning worked?"

"Yeah. It did. Sorry I'm late, though. I had a little something I needed to take care of first."

"You saw Leanne?" he guessed. It made sense. Daeva had a bond with the Cree woman.

She nodded. "I made sure the curse was gone. I figure I owed her that."

"You saved her life."

"I know. But she saved mine, as well. She was there in the abyss, she guided me home. To you."

He kissed her forehead, drinking her in, inhaling her scent, imprinting it into his psyche. "I thought you died."

"So did I." She shrugged. "Turns out it was

just a pit stop before this." She gestured with her hands to the kitchen. "I'm here now. For good. For as long as you want me."

"Is forever long enough?"

She nodded. "It's a start."

He wrapped his hands around her rear end, and picked her up to set her down on the counter. He settled himself in between her legs, his hands running through the long fall of her red hair. It was like silk on his skin.

"I've missed you," he murmured into the side of her neck.

She let her head fall back, exposing more of her throat to him. "Prove it," she teased.

He nibbled at her skin. "I'm going to spend the rest of my life proving it."

"Sounds good to me." She wrapped her legs around his waist and tugged him closer. "Now get busy. I'm still hungry."

Quinn claimed her mouth once more, eager to show her just how much he missed her. And just how much he was willing to do to prove to her that she was his everything and more.

* * * * *